CHRISTOPHER CARTWRIGHT

HABITAT ZERO

A SAM REILLY NOVEL

Copyright © 2018 by Christopher Cartwright
This book is protected under the copyright laws of the United States of America. Any reproduction or other unauthorized use of the material or artwork herein is prohibited. This book is a work of fiction. Names, characters, places, brands, media and incidents either are the product of the author's imagination or are used fictitiously. All rights reserved.

PROLOGUE

South Pacific Ocean–Two Weeks Ago

THE EXTRAVAGANT PLEASURE CRUISER TORE through the light blue waters surrounding the constellation of tiny islands and atolls that made up Micronesia as though it were a racecar. The ship had a length of two hundred and eighty feet, two helipads, a swimming pool with a retractable roof, and a sand-covered hydraulic platform that slid out of its port side right at the water line to create a perfect oasis. Not only did the floating oasis boast real sand and deck chairs, but also palm trees for a truly authentic experience. Inside, the ship was embellished with gold trimmings. It was the sort of overt and ostentatious show of wealth one would expect to see in a new class of new money—the mega rich of Silicon Valley.

She was owned by Travis Macintyre, whose digital startup was recently bought out by one of the bigger players for a sweet 1.2 billion dollars. Like the ship's name, *Carpe Diem,* the owner had seized the day with his unimaginable good fortune, bought the ship and filled it with every extravagant toy a kid could dream of, including a three person submarine, a small armada of jet skis, two helicopters and a seaplane.

Alicia Yeager stretched out along the front deck of the pleasure cruiser. She knew that she was just one of those expensive toys. She could have fooled herself into believing that Travis had fallen in love with her and one day the two of them would get married and have beautiful children. She had the looks and the guile to possibly even make it happen. But Travis wasn't the type of man she wanted to marry. He was still a kid and billionaires, she'd discovered, made the worst kind of kids.

No, she didn't want to marry Travis.

Oh, Travis adored her, all right. And why wouldn't he? She was twenty-five years old and had deep blue eyes and light brown hair. She had smooth, tanned skin and the sort of face that somehow formed the shape of a heart when she smiled. Just shy of six foot, she had small breasts, with a slim and athletic figure. She wore a tasteful, but scant bikini that accentuated her long legs. She smiled mischievously. Right now, he would give her anything she wanted, but she knew that when he got bored with her, she would be discarded like the rest of his used toys.

It didn't bother her. Travis was like no guy she'd ever met or was likely to meet again. It was like living in a dream, where she could go anywhere she wanted or do anything that took her fancy based on a whim. He was good looking, and good in bed, too. So why should it bother her that she knew it wouldn't last forever? Nothing lasts forever anyway, right?

The fine vibrations of the ship's powerful engines eased as they came to an idle. She felt the ship slow, and sat up. Ahead of them was an island covered entirely in white sand. She smiled, revealing a set of evenly spaced teeth like a model.

What's taken his fancy today?

She stood up, slid into a light see-through kaftan and made her way up to the bridge. Travis stood there studying the navigation table with James, the skipper. Travis was so engrossed by whatever he was studying that he didn't even notice her walk in.

After waiting for a moment to be noticed, she said, "What is it Travis? Where have you taken me today?"

Travis grinned. "I have no idea."

Alicia's eyes swept the small white island in front of her. She matched his smile. It was coquettish, calculatedly alluring. "No idea…where?"

"That's just it. I don't know."

"It looks nice," she said.

"Sure it does. But it doesn't belong here."

She shrugged. "What do you mean, it doesn't belong here? Islands don't just move, do they?'

"Not usually."

"But this one does?" she asked.

Travis opened a large admiralty map out onto the desk in front of her. With a pencil he made a marking of their current latitude and longitude on the map with an asterisk. "We're here. What do you see, Alicia?"

She studied the map. Despite her somewhat ditsy and playful persona, she was highly intelligent. Travis never would have fallen for her if she wasn't. He was rich enough to have a dozen beautiful strippers, but he wanted more than that. She could see clearly where they were, but there was a real difference between what she saw on the map and what was out the front of the bridge. In fact, it showed the *Carpe Diem* in the deep waters south of Guam, more than a hundred miles from any island. She glanced at the latitude and longitude displayed on the GPS and then noted the depth sounder—it read 1000 feet and had a plus symbol in front of it, which meant the real depth was greater than that amount—possibly much greater.

Alicia looked up at Travis, a genuine smile filled with curiosity spread along her face. "Where have you taken me, Travis?"

Travis studied the white island using binoculars. It was roughly the size of a football field and appeared flat, not more than a few feet high all over, with the exception of the middle section which was about ten feet. The island's shore was rolling in and out with each ripple of the gentle waves. He adjusted the focus on the binoculars and then smiled again. The shore wasn't just being swept by the waves; it was being gently lifted, too.

"What the hell is that?" He handed the binoculars to James. "Have you ever seen anything like this?"

James adjusted the binoculars, but remained silent.

Alicia asked, "When did you spot it?"

"About five minutes ago."

"You didn't see it earlier than that?"

"No."

"What about the radar?"

"It didn't spot it, either."

Alicia said, "What did it do, just turn up?"

"Yeah, something like that," Travis said. "It just popped up, and a new island was born."

She turned to James, "Well. What do you think it is?"

James smiled, and shook his head in disbelief. "It's not an island."

"Really?" Travis said. "It's much too big to be anything else. What do you think it is then?"

"Pumice!" James said.

Travis stared at the island in a new light. He could see it clearly now that his mind had gotten past its preconception. It was a sea of white volcanic stone and it wasn't an island. It was floating. "Let's bring her in closer for a look."

"You can't be serious?" James said.

Travis pushed the twin throttles forward and the pleasure cruiser eased forward. "Of course I am, why not?"

"It's probably not safe!" James and Alicia replied in unison.

"Of course it is. What's it going to do to us?"

Alicia shrugged. "What if the thing breaks apart?"

"It's not high enough to damage the *Carpe Diem*."

Alicia looked at James. "You want to tell him that he's acting like a fool?"

James shrugged. It wasn't his ship, and the man knew better than to contradict the owner and real master of the vessel.

"It's all right, Alicia." Travis eased the throttle back a little and glanced at the depth sounder. There was still more than a thousand feet beneath the hull. "I'll just take her in a little closer so we can get a better look. That's all."

"All right," Alicia said. She wrapped her arms around his waist and kissed the back of his neck with her soft lips. "Be careful, please."

"I will."

James idled the *Carpe Diem* in close to the shore until the portside of the pleasure cruiser rested against the floating pumice island. He pushed the throttles backward until the vessel slowed to a complete stop.

Alicia asked, "Now what?"

Travis smiled. "Now we go exploring."

Alicia watched as the sand-covered hydraulic platform was adjusted outward until it sat level with the waterline and the floating island of pumice. A slight crack in the island began to form where the bow wave of the large pleasure cruiser shifted the island. The water now settled back to its glassy stillness.

Travis stepped out of *Carpe Diem's* portside door, crossed the narrow, sandy platform and squatted down at the edge where sand now mingled with the pumice shore. He picked up a piece of pumice. It felt warm in his hand, but not too hot to touch. He threw it onto the island. The stone skipped along the top of the island for a few feet and then came to rest.

He smiled. It was a big movie star type of smile—full of evenly spaced teeth. Travis looked so happy. For a moment Alicia felt a pang of loss as she considered how beautiful their kids would have been if she did go against her own reservations and married the man. He then picked up a bigger stone and threw it onto the shore right next to them. It made her smile. He was just a big kid at heart. She took a step back, waiting for the splash.

The stone struck the floating island hard, but it didn't fall through as they were both expecting. Alicia glanced at Travis. His eyes were wide and his mouth open, as though he had discovered some tremendous idea, but wasn't quite certain how to put it into words yet.

"What are you thinking?" she asked.

Travis grinned. "It looks stable."

"Stable enough for what?"

"To walk on of course!"

Alicia frowned. "Are you sure that's safe?"

He spread his hands. "Sure, why not?"

"It might *not* be stable."

Travis shrugged.

"It's not like I can't swim. If I fall through I'll just swim back to you."

"Okay," she said, surprised by her own feelings of concern.

She watched as Travis moved along the artificial sandy beach looking for the thickest section of pumice shore. He paused after about ten seconds, and then jumped. His feet struck the pumice. The shore dipped a little and he wobbled, coming close to falling, but then balanced. Travis looked more like someone learning to surf for the first time. He was standing upright, but something about his posture gave her the impression it wouldn't be for very long.

The edge of the shore started to break apart, and he jumped further inland. This time the ground appeared as solid as any real island.

Travis grinned.

Alicia said, "Well?"

"Look at that, it holds my weight!"

"That's great." Alicia had only known the man for about two weeks, but sometimes she wondered how someone so rich could be so enrapt by something as simple as a pile of floating debris. She smiled; it was somehow a cross between coy and lascivious. "Now what?"

Travis made a show of standing up proudly to make a salute to an imaginary flag. "I claim this island in the name of the king, and call it, *Macintyre Island.*"

She smiled genuinely now. *Boys. So predictable.* "So what does that make you?"

"The king," he said. "Are you going to join me?"

She eyed the strange floating island, her eyes darting between the shore and the newly proclaimed king. "And then, pray tell, what does that make me?"

"My queen."

She clapped her hands. "In that case, I accept."

Alicia stepped lithely onto the island, skipping between the larger stones until she reached the deeper section where Travis now walked freely on thick layers of pumice. She caught up with the king, and he embraced her passionately. Their mouths met, and he kissed her. He could be dominating and commanding, but at the same time gentle, timid and unsure of himself. She felt him caress her back, running his fingers down her spine.

He stopped just short of her derriere and whispered in her ear, "Now, what shall we do on our island?"

She opened her eyes and met his sky gray colored eyes. "Anything you like. The island belongs to you, and so does everything on it."

Travis stepped back. "Good. In that case, I would like to

explore my kingdom."

She laughed. It was like dating a child. Alicia glanced around the island. "The place looks pretty barren to me. Did you have any ideas?"

"Over there!" He pointed toward the largest section of the island, where the pumice was at least ten feet thick, creating a small mound. "Let's climb it."

"Okay, you're the king."

"Race you to it!" Travis yelled, and started to run.

Alicia sprinted after him. It didn't take long, maybe a little under a minute to reach the small hill and race to the top. She trailed only a few feet behind him until he increased the gap as he pushed on through the thicker piles of pumice, and disappeared over the crest.

Her thighs burned as she climbed to the top, clearing the crest at a run. A split-second later, she felt Travis's muscular arms grab her and force her to the ground. There was no playfulness in his motion, nor was their malice. He'd done it to protect her. She fought him as he tried to keep her on the ground. But she'd been sunbaking before they'd discovered the island, so she wore sunscreen all over her body.

Travis struggled to keep a grip on her. She slipped away and faced him. "What the hell is it?"

"Don't look!" he shouted.

It was the sort of thing that inevitably made anyone look. Her eyes turned from his handsome face, into the opening at the center of the island. Alicia tried to comprehend what she was staring at. She tried to be strong, and keep her eyes fixed on it — but instead she found herself screaming, like some heroine in a badly acted seventies era horror film.

"It's okay," he was quick to comfort her.

She felt his warm arms wrap around her body, and in an instant she buried her head in his chest. She could have stayed there forever, protected from the sight, but instead she faced him, looking straight into his eyes. "No it's not. Nothing will ever be okay, again… will it?"

Alicia closed her eyes, but the image burned in her mind. The mound formed a hollowed crater like the inside of a volcano. It had a diameter of about forty feet and was at least ten deep. At the center were approximately five hundred birds. They were white all over with a black scalp. If either of them knew anything about migratory birds, they would recognize them as Arctic terns.

The birds had recently been made famous after the recognition of their lengthy migration. Arctic terns fly from their Arctic breeding grounds to the Antarctic and back again each year, across a minimal distance of 12,000 miles. They were amazing creatures, and right now, every one of them was dead. Not just dead — grotesquely damaged. Their eyes bulging out of their sockets, their bodies hideously deformed, blisters formed over their once cute little faces.

She opened her eyes and met Travis with a direct stare. "What do you think killed them?"

"I don't know. Most likely the gases. This is obviously some sort of volcanic ash, from an underwater volcano. It's pretty rare, but not unheard of. Maybe when it came up the gases killed the birds?"

"Do you think we're safe?"

"Of course we are," he said. "I remember hearing somewhere, probably on one of those Planet Earth documentaries or something, that pumice is formed by gas bubbles that were trapped in the rock during the rapid cooling of a gas-rich frothy magma. The material cools so quickly that atoms in the smelt are not able to arrange themselves into a crystalline structure. Thus, pumice is an amorphous volcanic glass. During the process of floating to the surface, the pumice would have been surrounded by intensely heated gas. The flock of birds must have been unlucky enough to be flying over at the time."

At times she forgot that underneath his boyish playfulness, lived a genius and a nerd. "How can you be so sure?"

"It would have been the heat that killed them. Now that the pumice and rest of the island has had time to cool and the hot gases dissipate, we should be perfectly safe."

"What if the gas is still around?"

He made a show of taking a deep breath. "Do you smell any gas?"

"No."

"Good. See, so it can't be still lingering. Besides, look where we are. The expanse of the open ocean is too great for any toxic gas to remain." His voice was confident, as his gaze swept their little island, before settling on her upset face. "Even so, we might head off, if you'd prefer."

She nodded, but said nothing, as she followed Travis back to the pleasure cruiser. Travis ordered the *Carpe Diem* to set a course to San Diego. She watched as James input the course into the ship's autopilot and the ship roared to life.

Travis turned to face her. "Are you all right?"

She nodded. "Just shocked, more than anything."

The boyish, playful expression of twenty minutes earlier was now replaced by sympathy and concern. He displayed a higher level of empathy than she expected. A level of warmth and comfort beyond his youth.

She smiled. In an instant, she realized that she could do a lot worse than marrying such a man. She made the conscious decision to say yes, if he ever asked.

"Would you like a drink?" he asked. "Something alcoholic, perhaps?"

She shook her head, feeling the start of a migraine coming on. "I think I might go to bed, I don't feel too well."

CHAPTER ONE

The 8th Continent, Pacific Ocean

THE US AIR FORCE LOCKHEED C-5 Galaxy flew in a southeasterly direction until it reached a section of calm seas a few hundred miles east of New Zealand. The massive military cargo transporter had a high wing with a distinctive high T-tail vertical stabilizer fin. Its four TF39 turbofan engines were mounted on pylons beneath wings that were swept 25 degrees as it soared above the Pacific Ocean.

Above its plane-length cargo deck was an upper deck for flight operations and for seating 75 passengers, including the embarked loadmaster crew, all who faced to the rear of the aircraft during flight. Cargo bay doors could be fully opened at the nose and tail to enable heavy vehicles to drive through the fuselage for loading.

Sam Reilly sat in the additional third seat in the massive cockpit and stared through the windshield at the sea below. It turned from its distinctive midnight blue of deep ocean waters through to the rich azure of the relative shallows.

He smiled at the sight and shook his head. It seemed impossible that the vast submerged landmass of the 8th Continent had remained hidden for so many years. He closed his eyes and imagined the place that he and Tom had discovered not so long ago. It belonged in a Jules Verne novel—a secret world, buried beneath the sea. To access it, they needed to navigate a submersible into a large underground grotto that used to be a volcanic atoll, but in the past fifty years had sunk to a depth of eighty feet. The entire beach, protected by a strange obsidian dome, remained filled with air.

The Air Force pilot pointed to the GPS waypoint. It was flashing, indicating that they were in close proximity to their desired location. The pilot turned to Sam. "We'll be overhead in ten minutes. Are you happy to be dropped in this water?"

Sam set his jaw firm and nodded. "Happy? No. Willing to out of necessity, yeah, why not?"

"Did you have another option, sir?"

"To reach the 8th Continent without others watching?"

The pilot nodded. "Yeah."

Sam said, "If the Secretary of Defense could have waited another couple of weeks, we would have been diving off my own vessel."

"You don't like my C-5 Galaxy?"

"No. I like your aircraft plenty." Sam suppressed a smile. "It's knowing that I'm going to have to wait a long time out here in the Pacific Ocean to be picked up after I complete my mission that concerns me."

The pilot shrugged. "I'm told you're to set off your encrypted EPIRB and a fishing vessel will be sent to retrieve you."

"That might take a few weeks."

The pilot laughed. "Hey, it was your idea."

"I know. I've been known to have some pretty stupid ideas every now and again." Sam stood up and patted the pilot on the shoulder. "Thanks for the ride."

"No problem. Good luck."

Then, to the copilot, Sam said, "You're sure we're high enough to deploy the Orcasub?"

"Certain, sir."

"All right, let's do this."

Sam left the cockpit, climbing down the steep set of internal stairs from the upper deck to the cargo deck below.

The loadmaster greeted him with a firm handshake. "Mr. Bower is already on board the Orcasub. He says the submarine's ready to be launched."

"Very good."

Sam followed the loadmaster aft, passed an Apache helicopter and two Military ATVs, before opening up to where the yellow sports submersible had been secured. The cargo crew were in the process of removing the MB-2 tie-down devices, rated at 25,000 pounds capacity each, in preparation for the airdrop.

Sam glanced at the submersible. Normally in the realm of multimillion-dollar toys of billionaires, it had become his predominant underwater reliable workhorse since the loss of the *Maria Helena* six months ago.

The loadmaster met his eye. "Good luck, sir."

Sam said, "Thank you."

He climbed on board and secured the hatch before moving forward into the cockpit.

Inside, he ran his eyes across the control settings. The buoyancy controls were all set to negative, meaning that the Orcasub would sink as soon as it hit the water. The batteries were all full and the power was switched on. All air tanks were within their highest boundaries.

He reached down and attached his headset, adjusting the mike so that it sat just below his mouth. Sam said, "How are we looking, Tom?"

"We're all set. The bathymetric map is all ready, and programmed into the system. All you have to do is follow the directions."

"Thanks."

Up ahead, the aft cargo bay door opened vertically.

Cocooned inside the airtight and confined space of the Orcasub, he felt nothing of the strong gust of air that wisped around the inside of the C-5 Galaxy's cargo deck. The aircraft reduced altitude until it looked like it was setting up to land on the calm water above the 8th Continent.

The loadmaster gave the thumbs up signal.

Sam reciprocated the signal and then on the internal radio, he said to Tom, "You'd better hold on, this is going to be a bumpy ride."

"Hey, I like the rides at Disneyland."

Sam gripped the brace bar with his left and right hand. "I don't think this is going to be like Disneyland."

The light next to the open cargo bay door turned from red to green.

Sam swallowed and pushed his body as hard into the seat as possible in an attempt to brace himself. The C-5 Galaxy flared just above the sea. A second later the loadmaster released the drogue chute. It shot through the cargo bay door and pulled the extraction chutes out into the airstream, opening fully with the loud crack of a whip.

The force of the extraction chutes immediately overcame the remaining floor lock, and the Orcasub was pulled out like the release of a catapult.

Sam's head jolted backward with the initial movement, but the landing was surprisingly soft, with the water absorbing much of the remaining force.

Behind them, the C-5 Galaxy was already climbing.

The submarine started to sink.

Sam blinked the haze from his sight and took control of the submersible with his right hand on the joystick.

"You okay, Tom?" he asked.

Silence.

Sam turned his head over his right shoulder, to get a visual of Tom. The man was grinning like an idiot.

"Tom! Are you all right?"

"All right?" Tom asked, his voice bemused. "That was the best ride I've had in a long time. What say we ask them to come pick us up for another go?"

"Forget about it. We've got things to do, and the Galaxy's never going to make a water landing."

"All right, all right," Tom accepted. "Let's go find out what Amelia Earhart found inside the 8th Continent."

CHAPTER TWO

SAM REILLY MANEUVERED THE SPORTS submarine with gentle, adept movements of the controls as he navigated the opening to the submerged world of the 8th Continent. The Orcasub was kind of a cross between an airplane and a two-seater submersible. Behind him, Tom Bower read out a series of intricate navigational details they had secured from their previous expedition, as a navigator would to a professional rally car driver.

The Orcasub set its course along a southwesterly direction through the remnants of an ancient submerged valley.

The submarine's exact dimensions were: 20 feet of length, 14 feet beam–with a 7-foot wingspan–and a height of 5 feet. There were two glass bubble domes positioned forward and aft of each other, where the pilot and copilot were housed. The overall shape of the submersible was sleek, like a sports-car, or more accurately, a sports underwater airplane, with narrow wings and a V-shaped tail-wing. The two wings even had two large thrusters fixed to each wing, like jet-engines on an aircraft.

Sam pulled back on the joystick, and the little submersible rose out of the higher cliffs of the nearly three-mile-wide valley, leveling out after its rapid ascent, across an ancient waterfall.

Emerging onto the tabletop of the 8th Continent.

The ancient river opened up to a shallow underwater plateau, covered in vivid and impressive coral gardens. It was a unique tropical playground that didn't belong anywhere near where they were. Coral reefs provided homes for tropical fish, sponges, mollusks, giant manta rays, sea turtles, and giant clams. The diversity of form and color was the sort of thing that inspired humanity to explore beneath the waves in the first place.

A small pod of dolphins raced ahead of their submersible, swimming upside down and by its side, like small torpedoes. Unlike last time they approached the secret submerged world, the dolphins seemed more wary of them, giving them a wider berth, before quickly losing interest and retreating into a series of small coral grottoes. It almost looked like they were scurrying away from danger.

Sam said, "Looks like they don't want to play today."

Tom gave a half-shrug. "They've seen us before. They probably have plenty of other fun creatures to play with in their undersea paradise."

"What could be more fun than a yellow submarine?"

"Good question." The muscles in Tom's face tightened. "I wonder if they've had another visitor since we were here last?"

"That's possible."

Sam put the thought out of his mind. There was nothing they could do about it currently.

His eyes swept their new environment with awe. The depth of the tabletop was roughly fifty feet, with a deeper narrow chasm through which the tiny submersible raced.

Sam gripped the joystick, easing the Orcasub up to a depth of 100 feet.

He said, "We're approaching the destination."

"I see it," Tom replied. "It's at your 3 o'clock position."

"Got it."

Sam slowed the Orcasub as he approached the end of the chasm, taking it to a stop at the mouth of a large underground chamber, roughly twenty feet high by thirty feet wide. He switched on the submarine's overhead lights, which shined like two little bug-eyes from the top of the sub. The cave formed out of the mouth of a small rocky outcrop on the coral tabletop, like an ancient monolith.

"You ready?" Sam asked.

Tom said, "Yeah. Take us in."

Sam dipped the joystick forward, and the Orcasub's propellers made a little whine as he edged her through the mouth of the opening.

The tunnel descended steeper until they were at a complete dive. At 160 feet, the rocky passageway appeared to level out, before ascending again.

At 140 feet the passageway opened, and seawater ceased. The submarine surfaced into a gigantic, air-filled grotto that extended so far back, that neither Sam nor Tom could see where it began or where it ended. A giant light filtered through the top of the cavern, like the rays of the sun, glistening onto the spectacular white beach.

Sam eased the Orcasub's throttles forward, until she became gently grounded on the sandy beach. Confident that the submarine was securely landed, Sam disengaged the hatch and climbed out. He removed his MP5 submachinegun and slung it over his shoulder. Tom climbed out second, carrying a rope and anchor behind him.

Sam fixed the anchor, burying it deep in the sand, while Tom attached the opposite end of the rope to a small retractable cleat on the Orcasub's starboard pontoon. After confirming the submarine was secured they made their journey along the same well-worn path they had taken previously. They meandered toward the half-dome shaped remnants of the ancient volcano that now overhung part of the beach like the mouth of a behemoth monster turned grotto.

They passed the wooden remains of a 16th century Dutch Fluyt and the intact, well-preserved remains of Amelia Earhart's Electra. They quickly reached the three pieces of obsidian, each as large as a bus, that jolted together to form a natural archway, and began their descent into the unique world below.

Sam stepped through the arched gateway.

A set of stairs had been carved into the brittle volcanic rock. It looked like a medieval stairwell, spiraling to the left with the precision that he doubted few stonemasons could recreate today. He moved with the determined gait of a professional soldier. His face set with an equal mixture of awe and curiosity, he descended deep into the subterranean tunnel.

Time quickly disappeared as they traipsed downward until light suddenly filtered through glassy rocks far below, allowing enough ambient glow to make out the shape of the tunnel and the location of the stairs, but little else.

The effort that someone had made to construct the strange stairwell amazed Sam. His ears hurt as he continued the descent, and he found himself swallowing to equalize them.

How far below sea level must we be?

He stepped around the next bend and his left hand came free of the cold stone wall. Sam stopped, his heart pounding in his chest. It was the second time he'd been down to the subterranean world, but nothing could prepare him for the sight ahead.

The stairwell ended on a giant rocky ledge that overlooked an underground prehistoric world to rival anything Jules Verne had imagined.

The ceiling in this new vault was so high that it could only be seen at the edges of the wall and not in the middle. A warm ray of sun shone down from above on the entire subterranean habitat, making him feel like he'd just stepped out into the great expanse of an ancient savannah. Giant trees and plants were covered with fruits filling his nostrils with the scent of rich fragrances.

His eyes swept the near-mythical environment with wonder. It was impossible to tell where the place began and where it finished. It might have been a small country in its own right. Thick rainforests, including giant gum trees, more than a hundred feet tall, filled the area. There were massive open plains of grass, and a freshwater river that split the ancient world in two, with multiple smaller tributaries and streams that ran off from it.

An 80-foot waterfall raged somewhere to the east, sending a fine mist down upon the valley. The sound of birds chirping echoed throughout. Ancient megafauna, oversized mammals and marsupials, drank by the bank of the river.

To his left, a beam of light filtered through the subterranean vault above, shining light the hue of purple, and lighting up the image like an exhibit at a museum — on seven faces of what looked like ancient cavemen. His eyes locked on the mysterious faces of the seven sub-species of the genus Homo, for which he now knew the Phoenix Plague had been created.

His gaze turned toward the clearing in the distance where the first sign of human habitation was evident with the appearance of a small hut nestled beside the river.

Sam and Tom headed into the jungle, toward a clearing near the river some three miles away. The sun was setting and they spotted a single light coming from a nearby cottage. It seemed rudimentary, more of the sort of place where Robinson Crusoe might have lived: a single-roomed log hut, with a waterwheel fed by the nearby stream, and a garden of remarkable flowers.

A woman was whistling a gentle tune inside.

Sam glanced at Tom, who shrugged.

He knocked on the door.

A woman opened it.

She was roughly 5 foot 8 inches, with a lanky build and

proportionate features. She wore a loose fitting cotton shirt, cargo pants, and leather boots. Her blonde hair, which was cut short, blew in the light breeze. She wore an impish smile, revealing a nice set of even white teeth, with a distinctive gap in the middle of her upper front incisors.

Sam took in a deep breath. "Amelia Earhart?"

The woman laughed. It was the sort of laugh Sam could get used to hearing. Full of joy and filled with life.

"No. She was my grandmother."

CHAPTER THREE

SAM GLANCED AT THE WOMAN'S face.

She had a nice smile. It was big and full of teeth. Her intelligent gray eyes were filled with life. If she was startled to see two strangers approach, she didn't show it. Her stance remained relaxed, her breathing natural and unlabored, her eyes leveling to meet them both with pleasure at their surprise at the extraordinary news.

Sam's grin turned incredulous. "You're Amelia Earhart's granddaughter?"

She nodded and offered her hand. "Jessica Earhart. But you can call me Jess."

Sam shook it. Her grip was firm and her hand strong. "Sam Reilly and this is…"

"Tom Bower," Jess said with a teasing smile. "I know. I was expecting both of you."

Tom said, "Pleased to meet you, ma'am."

Sam said, "How did you know who we were and that we were coming today?"

Jess dropped a large aluminum dog's bowl on the ground,

before opening a bag and emptying its contents of black pellet-like mash inside. She made a piercing whistle through pursed lips and shouted. "Rex, dinner time."

Sam glanced around the open yard toward the nearby cottage. It was the epitome of a domesticated agricultural society. A small farm with a series of exotic fruit orchards, a level field, a nearby stream — its water being captured by a large waterwheel and redistributed to the orchards of exotic fruits — and a small cottage with a domesticated dog by the looks of things. Not quite what he was expecting from the submerged prehistoric oasis.

"Rex! Dinner time." Jess looked around. She whistled again. "Where is that mutt?"

Sam frowned. "I'm afraid we didn't see a dog as we came in here."

Jess turned to face him again. Her face set with surprise, as though she'd only just recalled that two strangers from the topside had approached. "I'm sorry, what were you asking?"

"How did you know we were coming today?"

"Oh, that… we've been watching you for a while now."

"Really?"

Her voice softened. "Most of the inhabitants you see here are little more than a bunch of prehistoric troglodytes, but there are some who choose to live here, who are every bit as technologically advanced as you Topsiders… and we work together to ensure that our world isn't destroyed by its discovery."

Sam grinned. "Topsiders?"

She shrugged. "It's what we call you down here."

"We?" Sam asked. "How many people live down here?"

"I couldn't say exactly." She squinted her eyes and smiled, as though considering the question. "Somewhere in the vicinity of twenty thousand I think."

Sam gasped. "How far does the 8th Continent go?"

"It's nearly half the size of Australia, but its unique biosphere makes it far more fertile."

Tom frowned. "So why aren't there more humans down here?"

"Because it's a more balanced biosphere than you have above ground…"

"Meaning?"

"Human's aren't the only ones on top of the food chain."

Sam looked around, suddenly aware that his environment's megafauna may be lethal. For all intents and purposes he might as well be inside Africa's Serengeti, where more than just lions were currently in the process of stalking him. He gripped the hilt of his MP5 submachine gun as he recalled burrowing *Diprotodon,* a hippopotamus-sized marsupial most closely related to the wombat. It was thought to have become extinct 20,000 years ago in South Australia. He'd seen one on his last visit to the 8th Continent. The weapon's 9mm shots would be completely ineffective against such animals.

He made a somewhat nervous smile. "What is at the top of the food chain?"

"Homo Sapiens share that title with the Bunyip."

Sam's smile hardened. "The Bunyip… as in the large mythical creature from Australian Aboriginal mythology, said to lurk in swamps, billabongs, creeks, riverbeds, and waterholes?"

Jess smiled. "That would be the one."

"Seems unlikely that something out of the Aboriginal Dreamtime could keep the population numbers down in a place like this?"

"All enduring myths have a hint of truth to them," she countered. "What do you know about the Bunyip?"

Sam recalled early stories from his childhood when he spent time in the Blue Mountains near Sydney, Australia, where his mother had grown up. "The word Bunyip is usually translated by Aboriginal Australians today as devil or evil spirit."

"That's right. Do you remember what it looks like?"

Sam closed his eyes for a moment, searching his memory, but finding nothing but blanks. "No. It wasn't anything. The Bunyip was a fictional creature to frighten children."

"And yet for the Australian Aboriginals it was very real."

"Yes."

"It's actually a Diprotodon."

There was something that Sam could remember. "But Diprotodon was the largest marsupial to ever live. If I recall correctly, it was a hippopotamus sized cross between a koala and a wombat—and a herbivore."

"That's right."

"So how does a herbivore become an apex predator?"

"Through genetic anomalies."

"Meaning?"

"While the introduction of Homo sapiens into the continent of Australia nearly 50,000 years ago caused the extinction of the Diprotodon, the oversized marsupial evolved into a carnivore."

Sam said, "But the Diprotodon hasn't been wiped out here. We've seen them in the wild, eating from the vegetation."

"That's right."

"Then where does the Bunyip come from?"

"It's a genetic anomaly."

Sam glanced over his shoulder. "So should we be worried about a stray Bunyip?"

"Not right now. Like the Diprotodon before them, they are nocturnal, but we'll have to find someplace high up tonight to sleep."

"We?"

"Yes. Of course. I'm coming with you."

Sam said, "I think it's time you explain how your grandmother came to be a resident of the 8th Continent…and what happened to your own parents?"

"It's a long story. But I'll explain on the way."

"Way?" Sam asked. "Where?"

Jess opened her mouth to answer, but Sam didn't hear what she had to say. Instead, his attention drifted across the field. The dense vegetation on the bank of the nearby stream started to ruffle and part as though something was forcing its way through. Sam's gaze darted toward the parting prehistoric bushes. It looked like something was making its way to them, running at full speed. Whatever it was, it sure as hell wasn't a dog.

Sam's eyes narrowed, his vision fixed on the edge of the clearing. He glanced at Jess, but she seemed either unaware or unperturbed by the approaching beast. He restrained his emotions, forcing himself to slow his breathing as he listened to what was coming for them, but he heard little over the thump of his heart pounding in the back of his head.

The outline of a strange creature appeared through the scrub, racing toward them, its speed so fast that it looked like little more than a blur.

Sam switched his MP5 submachinegun from *Safe* to *Fully Automatic.*

He held his breath and aimed the weapon at the fast approaching beast — a sheep-sized echidna with spikes nearly a foot long running up its back.

Jess pressed her hand on his weapon, forcing him to lower it, "Stop!"

Sam took a step back, tilting the barrel toward the ground, but able to be lifted and fired at a split second's notice.

Tom reached for his MP5 submachinegun.

"Stop Rex!" Jessica turned to Tom and with both hands outward, she waved at him placatingly. "Don't shoot!"

The ancient sheep-sized echidna stopped mid-stride.

"Good boy, Rex."

Sam expelled a breath of air. "What the hell is that?"

Jess smiled. "That's Rex—AKA an oversized echidna, once part of the predominant megafauna in Australia roughly forty thousand years ago, until the introduction of *Homo sapiens* wiped them out in under a century."

Sam said, "And you trained it?"

"Trained it?" Jessica laughed. "More like it domesticated me. They're very intelligent creatures, affectionate too, but extremely protective of their owners—thus it wanted to come at you when it saw you approach me."

Tom said, "You're lucky we didn't kill it."

"Kill it!" she said. "How could you have even thought about harming such a creature?"

"Well, for a start, the thing looks like it weighs about a ton, and second its covered in spikes, and third, it was running at us at full speed like a Mac Truck."

Jess shrugged. "They're harmless to humans."

Sam raised his eyebrows. "Really? Because I didn't feel that way."

"I wouldn't worry. It was more likely to just try and lick you to death than inflict any real damage. Hey Rex, come here and say hello to our guests."

The echidna turned at the sound of her voice and started heading toward Sam and Tom, its nose twitching side to side as it soaked in their unique scent. It stopped directly in front of Sam, extended its giant tongue out of its snout and gave him an incredibly sticky lick on the hand.

Sam slowly pulled his hand away. "Hey… pup… nice to meet you."

Rex nuzzled into him abruptly, knocking him over.

Sam pushed back, trying to brush the massive creature out of his way with his arm, and the echidna rolled onto its back, revealing a soft fur-like tummy.

Sam rolled his eyes. "It wants to play dead?"

Jess shook her head. "No. It wants a rub on its belly."

Sam's lips curled into a bemused grin. "Your lethal prehistoric animal thinks it's a dog?"

"Yeah, not only can it retrieve things, but it follows complex orders..." The bottom of Jess's lip curled inward and she bit it as though suppressing a beaming smile. "Most of the time, unless it gets distracted — which is often — and in that way it's like a dog."

"Well, now I can say I've really seen it all," Sam said, grinning.

Tom shifted his MP5 cautiously back into safe mode.

Sam leaned down to pat the ancient echidna. Rex nuzzled him and Sam patted the echidna in the soft fur beneath its snout. The creature responded with a sound that bordered on the resonant purr of a relaxed cat.

Jess gave Rex a pat and said, "Okay boy, you can go eat now."

Rex gave a quick snort, and ran toward the dinner bowl. His nearly three-foot-long snout appeared like a cruelly misplaced anomaly on the otherwise fearsome looking creature, as it dipped into the bowl and sucked up the black mash.

Sam wondered what one fed such an oversized monotreme to eat.

Instead, his mind returned to the question of how the granddaughter of the famed aviator, Amelia Earhart, ended up marooned in the submerged continent.

He asked, "What happened to Amelia? How did you get here?"

"All in due time. I'll fill you in about everything along the way."

"Way? You said that before," Sam said, taking in a deep breath. "Where are we going?"

Jess glanced up at the sun overhead, which had a strange

purple hue to it. "It's getting late. We really should go now."

Sam said, "Where?"

She laughed, "To meet the Master Builders, of course."

Sam's eyes narrowed. "You know about the Master Builders?"

"Yes, that's why you've come here, isn't it?"

CHAPTER FOUR

JESSICA EARHART SAT DOWN BESIDE her oversized pet echidna. She gave it a good pat beneath its snout. "I'm going away for a few days, Rex. Be sure to look after the place while I'm gone, okay?"

Rex's narrow eyes, almost black in appearance, seemed to sadden. He nuzzled his way underneath her arm, placing his spiky head on to her lap and staring up at her with adoration. She stroked the creature's face, and its spikes relaxed into a downward position, allowing her to run her hands safely along its back.

"It's all right; I promise I won't be any longer than I have to." She turned to point toward Sam and Tom. "These gentlemen have come a long way to meet someone, and it's important I take them to make sure they get there safely."

Rex stared at her curiously.

"Where have they come from?" she asked.

Rex nuzzled her in acknowledgment.

"They're topsiders."

Rex sat up, as though suddenly wary, his spikes pointing

straight up.

Jess stroked the soft fur beneath his snout again until he settled. "It's okay, Rex. They're good people. They've come to see the Gifted Ones. I won't be long."

Rex blinked, his eyes set in doleful acceptance.

Sam asked, "Gifted Ones?"

"It's what people around here call the Master Builders." She stood up and gave Rex one last pat. "Take care of things while I'm gone, Rex."

Rex made a trilling whistle sound.

"I know you do, Rex. You always look after the place for me." She turned to Sam and Tom. "Are you guys ready to leave?"

"Sure," they both replied in unison.

Sam said, "How far are we going?"

She shrugged. "About three to four days hike, depending on whether or not the two of you can keep up."

"Right," Sam said, adjusting the straps on his backpack. "We're good to go as soon as you're ready."

"Ready?" Jess asked. "I'm already good to go."

"Don't you need to pack supplies or something?"

She shook her head and made an impish smile. "No. I'm good."

Sam raised his eyebrow with incredulity. "You're going away for a week with nothing?"

"Yeah. Why? What do you think I need?"

"I don't know. How about food and water?"

"This place provides everything we need. I'll explain as we go."

Sam shrugged. "Okay. We'll follow you."

"I'll just lock the door to the cottage. Rex is pretty good at keeping stray monotremes from wandering inside, but if we're going to be away for a while, I should make sure it's secure."

Sam suppressed a grin. "Sure. Do whatever you need to do to keep oversized wildlife from taking over your habitat."

Jess walked quickly toward the cottage. She took a small glance across her shoulder to make certain that Sam and Tom weren't following her.

She opened the building's single door and adjusted the intricate wooden lock so that it secured when she closed it again.

Jess's eyes traced the outline of the single roomed wooden cottage. Starting at the kitchen, she confirmed that the single fire was indeed out and there was no meat left on the smoking rack above it. The windows were all bolted shut.

Her eyes settled on a dark figure at the farthest corner of the room.

She held her gaze there for just a moment. About to turn around and leave, the figure moved. She stopped, holding the door open slightly; her eyes darted toward Sam and Tom — who were outside being convinced to play fetch with her pet echidna. Her eyes returned to the man at the end of the room.

He was struggling to move his arms and legs. Bound by thick kangaroo hide the man had almost managed to slip the gag off his mouth.

Jessica frowned, and moved quickly toward him.

She shifted the gag upward, adjusting it so that it bound her captive's mouth harshly, cutting into the soft skin around his lips and cheeks.

The man opened his eyes wide in terror, as though they could scream in place of his gagged mouth.

They were a deep purple color.

And they watched her as she turned and walked out of the cottage, closing the door behind her.

Jess met Sam and Tom and all three of them headed south, deeper into the submerged world of the 8th continent.

Sam fell into step next to her. "You said that the Gifted Ones wanted to speak to me?"

"Yes," she said, without changing her stride.

"Why?"

She made a suppressed grin. "I don't know, but if I had to guess… I'd say they need your help."

CHAPTER FIVE

JESSICA DIDN'T WAIT TO ELABORATE.

Instead, she set the pace with a determined stride as they headed deeper into the mysterious submerged world of the 8th Continent. Sam kept up with her, walking at a fast pace, while Tom settled behind them, taking in their new environment, constantly scanning it for signs of danger.

The trail followed the river as it meandered in a southeasterly direction. Eucalyptus regnans trees, more than three hundred feet tall, lined the river, casting dark shadows across the valley to the west. The ancient trees were the world's second largest, surpassed in height only by the California Giant Sequoia trees. Above, the purple hue of the sun pierced the horizon, turning the sky dark purple.

"What's up with your sunlight?" Sam asked.

Jess turned her palms skyward, making her lips form an intentionally coy smile. "What about it?"

"It's not natural is it?"

Jess glanced at the purple hue of the setting sun on the horizon. "Oh, that… you know, having been born down here, the orange thing that you topsiders have, seems strange to me."

Sam thought about that for a moment. "That makes sense. I still wonder why? I mean, where did the Gifted Ones draw the sunlight from? And what makes it that unnatural purple color?"

"Oh, that I can answer. Violet is at one end of the spectrum of visible light, between blue and the invisible ultraviolet. It has the shortest wavelength of all the visible colors. It is the color the eye sees looking at light with a wavelength of between 380 and 450 nanometers…"

Sam said, "How the hell did you work all that out down here?"

"My mother was an engineer, like her mother before her. She explained it to me years ago. Basically, it has to do with the way the light is drawn in through the obsidian, filtering out all visible light with the exception of the color purple before ultraviolet takes its place."

"Wow…" Sam suppressed a smile. Despite growing up in a prehistoric world, she was well educated in science and technology. "Good answer."

Jess stopped and pointed at the large river. "That's the Sentinel River. It divides this entire continent in half. The Gifted Ones who want to speak to you live on the peak of a mountain roughly fifty miles south of here."

Sam said, "That doesn't sound too far."

"It is when you're walking through the 8th Continent."

Sam's eyes narrowed. "Why?"

"It can be a dangerous place. There are no roads or well-worn trails to follow. No straight lines. We have to constantly alter our directions to achieve our navigation goals."

Tom asked, "Why don't we build a raft and take the river?"

Jess shook her head. "You don't want to get too close to this river."

Tom grinned. "Why not? Does it have crocodiles?"

"Yeah, but you don't have to be afraid of those so much. They keep to themselves. It's the bunyips that are deadly."

Sam said, "I thought bunyips were nocturnal?"

"They are. But the enormous canopies of the variety of forests that dwarf the Sentinel make some parts of the river permanently fixed in darkness—and bunyips come out in darkness."

They continued walking due south.

Sam said, "Tell me more about the 8th Continent."

Jess smiled. "What do you want to know?"

"Everything."

She laughed. "You might want to be a little more specific."

"All right. How big is it? Can you describe its topography? What sort of civilization lives here?"

"Okay." She closed her intelligent gray eyes for a moment, as though considering where to start, and then opened them, fixing her gaze on Sam. "From what I've been told, it's roughly half the size of the Australian continent. The entire place is one giant dome biosphere. The Sentinel River is the entire continent's primary source of fresh water and splits the dome in two. It runs in a clockwise direction following a roughly south, to west, to north, to east course."

Sam cocked an eyebrow. "The same river runs around in a circle?"

"Afraid so."

"Why?"

Her eyes narrowed. "Why what?"

"What makes it go around?" Sam asked. "I mean, a normal river is fed by gravity, always trying to reach the lowest point, before eventually settling on a level equilibrium when it meets the ocean. So what drives this one to go around in a giant circle?"

Jess shrugged. "Beats me."

Sam's lips twisted in an incredulous smile. "Weren't you

curious?"

"Sure I was." She folded her arms across her chest. "But some things about this place I have never been able to explain using my knowledge of science. My guess is that the Gifted Ones built this place so that a magnetic pulse drives the river from the south back to the higher grounds of the north, where gravity can once again allow it to flow. But that's just a guess. People have looked for a mechanical pump, or some sort of mechanical device used to drive the water up hill, but no one's been able to locate such a thing. It's like the entrance to this place..."

"The entrance?" Sam asked. "What about it?"

"Well, we're more than a thousand feet beneath the surface of the ocean. So why doesn't water flood the entire biosphere?"

Sam grinned. "I had the same thought, but shrugged it off, guessing that the dome shaped entrance created a natural S-bend like that used in plumbing."

"It does. But the pressure from the ocean above should have been powerful enough to smash through that air plug. No, the Master Builders have used ancient technology, beyond our feeble minds to artificially increase the pressure down here, so that the seawater is prevented from penetrating and flooding in."

Sam considered the hydro physics, but couldn't justify any of it on scientific grounds and the laws of physics. He filed the thought in his memory banks under topics to discuss with a hydrologist. "Can you tell me more about the landscape?"

"What you see here is the most densely populated section of the biosphere. The land is highly fertile, providing all our daily needs without any need for cultivation or agriculture. Wild plants provide an abundance of edible berries, trees grow fruits and nuts, and wild animals are plentiful. It rains regularly, the sun shines bright, and life simply thrives. Most of the civilization lives within a hundred miles of where we're standing."

A cold gust of wind blew across them. "What about the

wind?"

"You don't have wind on the topside?"

"Sure we do. But we also have the entire surface of Earth, with four seasons, causing a constant change globally in terms of rising warm air and falling cold air, which creates wind. If this is indeed a domed biosphere, there shouldn't be any wind at all."

"I think you underestimate the size of this biosphere." Jess made a superior smile, as though she was enjoying his ignorance. "There are four distinct seasons here on the 8th Continent. Unlike in the topside, these lands don't rotate through any of them. Instead, here, in the most fertile area, we live in permanent spring. There is an equal amount of rain and sun, and as you can feel, the air is warm. More than ninety-five percent of the inhabitants live in this quadrant."

"You call your land a quadrant?"

"Yeah." Her voice was soft, intrigued. "What else should I call it?"

Sam gave that some thought. "I don't know. I suppose I'm having difficulty grasping what this land looks like. I wish I had a map."

Jess stopped. In the sandy shore of the river, she picked up a smooth river stone and drew a big circle. "This is the 8th Continent."

Sam glanced at the circle. "Okay."

She drew a vertical line and a horizontal line through the middle, spitting it into four separate quadrants. "Humans and most animals for that matter can live in the two northern quadrants. Fall in the northwest and spring in the northeast. For the most part, people choose to live here in the northeast."

"And the two southern quadrants?"

"Animals do live there. Heck, even some humans have been, but it takes a lot more effort and struggle to survive. You have to remember the seasons don't rotate down here, so summer is permanent and so is winter. In the south west, the land has hundreds of miles of scorching desert, a wasteland where almost nothing can survive, before ending in a land with a permanently active volcano — a place filled with lava lakes."

Jess looked up at him, apparently waiting for some sort of challenge.

Sam merely waited in silent acceptance, before saying, "Go on. What about the winter quadrant?"

She sighed slowly. "The icy southeast quadrant is frozen all year round, with hundreds of miles of icy plains, before a high rising mountain."

"Have you ever been outside this quadrant?"

"I've been to the northwest, but never to the south."

"So then, how do you know what it's like in the south?" Sam asked.

"Because I've seen detailed maps."

"Really? Where?"

"The same place we're headed." She sighed heavily, as though she knew her next words were going to sound crazy. "At the center of the maze."

CHAPTER SIX

SAM STARED AT HER, DOUBT fixed on his face. "You're taking us to the center of a maze?"

"Yeah, I know what it sounds like, but it's the truth," Jess said.

She smiled and started walking down the trail again in silence.

"What sort of maze? Where is it?"

"It's constructed from a combination of dense forest and obsidian. The maze is south of here... toward the center of the spring quadrant."

Sam exchanged glances with Tom who looked relaxed, like he was really taking in the view of the crystal-clear river as it flowed casually to the south. Tom grinned. Sam could read his expression clearly—it said, *you're the one who wanted to go explore the 8th Continent.*

Sam turned to Jess. "So why are you taking us to the maze?"

"Because that's where the Gifted Ones are waiting for you."

Sam squinted beneath the bright purple sunlight. "The Master Builders live at the center of a maze?"

"Yeah, there's an open area, full of livestock and agriculture designed to support the Gifted Ones, and a big sandstone colonial house in which they live. It's the only place inside the 8th Continent with dedicated agriculture. It's a mini utopia. A place where one's safety is assured. The maze prevents all predators from entering."

"Why?"

"To serve the Master Builders who live there."

The gradient of the trail increased in a downward direction, until Sam had to dedicate all of his attention to climbing rather than talking.

When he reached the leveled river again, he asked, "What humans live here?"

"There are three distinctly different groups of Homo sapiens that live down here. The Gifted Ones — those who you call the Master Builders. There aren't many and they tend to come and go. To the ancient Homo sapiens, Gifted Ones are seen as Gods. The majority of the human inhabitants originate from Australia, having broken free from the southern continent more than fifty thousand years ago. There are roughly twenty thousand who live here."

Sam asked, "What are they like?"

"I would consider them a hybrid species."

"In what way?"

"They're hybrid. They evolved along the same path as you and I, but haven't had the same resources as those on the surface. More importantly, they've had everything they needed to fulfill their daily needs here, without much need for cultivation of the land for agriculture."

"You mean, they haven't evolved out of necessity?"

"Genetically they're identical to you and I. The difference is, roughly ten thousand years ago, when our ancestors were starting to settle down and domesticate plants and animals at the founding of the agricultural age, they didn't."

"I wonder why?"

"Their environment is already plentiful. There was no need for them to change their hunter-gatherer lifestyle."

"So they're entirely primitive? They really are just a bunch of troglodytes?"

"No. They've developed in their own way. Art, culture, literature, science. But not like those on the topside. There is no oil down here, so the internal combustion engine was never invented, the clement weather is permanent, so there has been little need to develop synthetic clothing to keep warm, or structures in which to reside. In many ways, they are evolutionarily equivalent to those of the 18th century, with a much higher development in literature and philosophy. Even more interesting, still, is the fact that if you were to show them complex machinery from the surface, they would grasp the foreign concepts faster than you and I and quickly become capable of reproducing it."

"Why?"

"Beats me. Just the way they've evolved, I guess. Maybe their brains aren't being tested. Or maybe because they haven't atrophied by the constant assistance of technology. I don't know."

Sam watched a couple large, flightless birds running across a field on the opposite side of the river. They looked like emus, only much larger.

"Have you been to the surface?" he asked, his voice suddenly serious.

"No, never."

"Then how do you know so much about it?"

"My grandmother brought a couple of books on her flight…"

"Really? I would have thought Amelia Earhart wouldn't have had much room for books, particularly when weight was such an issue. Besides, she disappeared in 1937, well before a lot of the technology you're talking about was developed."

Jess's cheeks flushed and she made a coy smile. "The Gifted Ones have a giant library from the world above. As an outsider, I've been allowed to visit. I spent my life reading about science and the world above."

"And yet you've never wanted to leave this place?"

"No. I've read enough to know that what we have here is a sort of utopia, long forgotten on the surface."

They continued walking south in silence, following a trail that ran alongside the river. By late afternoon the river entered a deep ravine, the height of which seemed to rise as the distance between the near vertical edge of the ravine and the river seemed to narrow, until the trail split into two — with one branch turning toward the river where a manmade jetty had been built, and the other blending into the cliff-like rise of the valley wall.

Jess paused for a moment as though deciding which direction would be faster to take. Sam dropped his backpack, ready to have a short break. Then, without discussing anything with Sam or Tom she took the path to the left and started to climb. Sam made a quick exchange with Tom, who merely shrugged as if to say, *I'm game if you are.*

Sam met Tom's eye. "She looks like she's in some kind of hurry."

Tom shrugged. "First time she's met a stranger from the topside, and she doesn't have any time to answer any number of questions. Go figure."

Sam adjusted his backpack, and continued after her. "What do you make of her, Tom?"

"She seems lovely. A spitting image of her grandmother."

"Right. That's what I thought." Sam watched her gracefully navigate a series of steep boulders. "Does that seem strange to you?"

"What?" Tom grinned. "That she looks like her grandmother?"

"Exactly. Where are her father and grandfather's DNA?"

"I don't know. Maybe she'll explain… when we can catch up with her."

"If you were the granddaughter of one of the most extraordinary aviators in history, who mysteriously disappeared, wouldn't you want to tell that story to the first person you met?"

"Exactly," said Tom.

"But she doesn't seem to have any interest in telling her story."

"What are you suggesting, Sam?"

"That maybe she's not being all that truthful. That she has an alternative reason for bringing us deeper into this submerged world…"

Tom laughed. "Like the Sirens of ancient Greek Mythology whose voice lured nearby sailors to shipwreck on the rocky coast of their islands?"

Sam shrugged. "Okay, probably not quite right… but I still don't know what to make of her."

"Neither do I." Tom met his eye. "You want to turn around and call it quits?"

Sam arched an eyebrow. "And miss out on finally finding the truth about the Master Builders?"

Tom shrugged. "It's your call."

"Hell no. We'll follow her to the end."

CHAPTER SEVEN

Sam tightened the strap for his backpack.

He took in a deep breath of air and followed Jess as the trail turned upward, where a series of small hand holds had been painstakingly carved into the granite side. Sam ran his eyes upward, tracing the imperceptible grooves that outlined the trail as it ran along the cliff before eventually heading upward some two hundred feet above.

He swallowed the fear that rose in his throat like bile. He'd never liked heights, and had a particular aversion to falling from them. But it didn't matter. He'd come here to find the truth about the Master Builders and some risks had to be taken.

Sam progressed up the vertical trail, shifting his hands from each individual hand hold, purposely placing each hand and foot and testing it until he was certain it could support his weight before he moved on to the next one.

Over the course of the next two hours Sam made his way gradually higher on the cliff as it followed the river, until he was looking out onto the tops of the great Eucalyptus regnans trees.

Up ahead, Jess stopped on a small ledge long enough for

them to catch up.

Sam paused, gritting his teeth as he prepared for the most dangerous traverse—exposed to more than two hundred and fifty feet of air below him.

Jess glanced at him, her mouth parting in an impish smile. "You don't like heights, do you?"

Sam grinned. "Sure I do—just from the cockpit of a helicopter."

Jess sat down so her legs were hanging off the ledge. "I'm afraid we don't have any of those down here, although I'm sure my grandmother would have loved them."

"I'm sure she would have." Sam gripped the hold carved into the wall behind the ledge and pulled himself up, keeping his hands clamped over the rock tightly, and his back wedged up against the wall of granite.

Behind him, Tom shuffled across the traverse, hanging onto the carved rocky handholds with the comfort of a kid playing on the monkey gym. When he reached the ledge he stood upright, without holding onto anything, staring at the view across the river and out to the plains far into the horizon. His eyes landed on Sam. "How are you doing?"

Sam expelled a deep breath. "I've been better. I'd like to know how in the thousands of years people have lived down here, no one has thought to invent ropes to make this sort of climbing safe."

"It is safe," Jess argued. "Just don't fall."

"Sure." Sam backed into an opening in the rock at the end of the ledge, formed between the main granite rockface, and a broken flake—a thin slab of rock detached from the main face— that extended another thirty feet higher, revealing a narrow chimney in between. "On that subject, do you want to tell us where we're heading from here?"

Jess grinned. "I'm ready to answer any questions you may have about my grandmother and about this submerged world…

if you'd like."

"Oh, now you're interested in talking."

"Sure," Jess replied, kicking her knees up back and forth across the open expanse to stretch them. "I need to catch my breath."

Sam squeezed deeper into the chimney, feeling safer compressed between the two giant pieces of stone. His eyes darted around, searching for the next set of carved hand holds. "I'm going to take a raincheck on that. You mind telling us where we go from here?"

"Isn't it obvious?"

"No."

Jess turned her eyes upward. "I think it is."

Sam followed her gaze. "We have to climb up this stone chimney?"

"Afraid so. It's the only way to reach somewhere safe before night fall. Why else did you think I was racing to get here?"

"Why? What's going to kill us after nightfall?"

She shrugged. "The more relevant question is, what's not going to kill us after nightfall?"

"Really?" Sam said.

Jess nodded. "Afraid so."

Tom met her eye with defiance. "We're well armed to defend ourselves against whatever predators live here."

"Your BB-guns won't do much against the large apex predators that roam this place at night."

Sam refused to be pulled into her superstitious fears. "So then, where are we headed?"

"Like I said, we climb."

Sam took a deep breath and stood up. "All right, then let's climb."

CHAPTER EIGHT

Skyway of the 8th Continent

SAM WATCHED AS JESS ADEPTLY maneuvered her body up the tight granite chimney.

Tom said, "You want me to go next?"

Sam shook his head. "No way. I need you below me in case I fall. I figure you might just be big and ugly enough to break my fall if something goes wrong."

Tom shrugged. "Glad I can help."

Sam placed his left foot forward onto the granite flake and his right leg backward. Using a technique popular with rock climbers called stemming, he began his ascent of the chimney. The concept was to place your hands and feet on opposite ends of the rock walls and push outwards as though trying to push through.

Maintaining as much external pressure as possible, Sam stood up, supported by his legs. He shuffled upward, shifting his weight from each foot to ascend using his hands primarily for balance. Apart from the risk of a life-threatening fall if he slipped, the process was quite simple and didn't require much effort compared to traditional rock climbing.

At the top, Jess was waiting for him.

He gripped a large hand hold dug into the top of the flake, finding its bucket-like presence reassuring, as he pulled himself to the top.

Taking a deep breath in, his eyes swept the environment.

A bridge made of cordage rope ran from the top of the flake through to a network of bridges that spanned the trees of the high rising forest, before reaching a treehouse built at the crest of an ancient Eucalyptus regnans nearly three hundred feet above the river.

Sam sighed. At least the bridge looked like it was well constructed, with railings and cross-bracing. Jess stood up to start making her way along the bridge.

Sam asked, "What is this place?"

"We call it the skyway," she replied. "It's the safest way to cross the river and also to travel south toward the maze."

"What makes it safer?" Sam asked, testing the strength of the upper rung of the rope balustrade.

"Predators come out at night. That's why it's important to be up high before nightfall."

"Most people live in treehouses?"

"They do out here."

"But not where you live?"

"No. Bunyips and other predatory creatures don't travel that far north. They live in dormant water, not the fast-flowing start of the Sentinel River. On that subject, we should get going; it's not safe to stay still up here in the daylight."

"Why not?"

Jess didn't answer. Instead, she started to move along the skyway, with the same sort of speed and fervor as she had used along the river's trail.

Sam's eyes darted from her to Tom. "It's not safe up here in the daytime. What the hell does that mean?"

"Who knows…"

Sam said, "Are you right to keep going?"

Tom unslung his MP5 submachinegun and switched it to rapid fire. "In for a penny, in for a pound."

"Good man."

Sam tested the bridge once more and then followed Jess out into the skyway, high above the open expanse below. It didn't take long for him to gain confidence in the system of adjoining ropes, and although far from confident, he was able to move along with speed.

He watched Jess up ahead with new interest.

Something had changed as soon as she'd reached the skyway. The difference was subtle at first, but now seemed dramatic. He tried to question her about it, but she shrugged it off, simply telling him and Tom to keep moving.

But he couldn't dismiss the change.

Jess had taken on a more serious demeanor for the first time. Her insouciance while climbing the granite staircase was replaced with resolute determination, and a vigilant alertness he'd not seen previously. Her eyes darted from side to side of the bridge, upward and downward, as though scanning for some unseen predator.

They crossed more than twenty bridges, which seemed to form a superhighway above the Sentinel River, before stopping for a brief moment to grab a drink of water from a wooden mechanical contraption that drew ice cold water from the river below.

Jess splashed some over her face and then kept going.

She got halfway across the next bridge before Sam spotted the predator approach from the sky!

He looked up, and yelled, "Run!"

CHAPTER NINE

———ıı∞⟨✕⟩∞ıı———

JESS EITHER DIDN'T HEAR HIM, or couldn't see where the bird of prey was coming from. Either way, the creature was diving straight at her.

Sam raced across the bridge, running at full speed.

The massive bird descended at a freefall like a bomb being dropped from a plane high above. Its huge wings were arched backward as its velocity continued to rise. Behind him he heard the rapid-fire burst of shots from Tom's MP5.

The shots missed.

Jess turned to face him. The lips of her mouth parted in surprise. "What?"

Sam dived at her, knocking her over.

The bird turned at the last moment, its massive talons swooping down inches above their heads.

Jess recovered quickly, rolling Sam over so that she could regain her feet. "Quick! It will make another attempt!"

Sam stopped. Dropped his backpack and removed his own weapon from his shoulder, switching it to rapid fire.

Tom said, "Can you see it?"

"No." Sam's eyes swept the air above. "Where the hell is it?"

Jess stood next to the massive trunk of the Eucalyptus regnans. With a diameter of fifteen feet, the trunk formed a solid wall of hardwood. "Quick! Get out of the open!"

Sam ran his eyes across the sky above. Failing to see anything, he glanced at Tom. "Come on, let's go!"

Tom nodded and lowered his weapon.

They raced to the protection of the tree.

"It can't swoop us here. When it dives it reaches speeds of nearly eighty miles an hour. If it tried to do that here, it would most likely kill itself in the process."

"Could it come in slower?" Sam asked.

"Sure it can, but it's the speed that makes it lethal. If it tries to grab one of us with its talons at low speed, we'll be able to fight if off — unless it gets lucky."

"And then?"

"One of its talons might just sever an artery in one of our throats."

Sam was breathing hard. Blood pounded in the back of his head. "What's the chance of it trying that?"

"Low… unless it's hungry."

"And then?"

"It will try anything until it gets what it wants. That's the problem with apex predators; they don't know when to stop."

"Right…" Sam searched the sky above. There was nothing.

Tom looked across to the opposite end of the bridge. "Could it have simply given up after its first attempt?"

Jess shook her head. "If it has, it would be the first time."

Sam asked, "What the hell is it?"

She raised her finger to her lips. "Don't speak. They have excellent hearing."

Sam and Tom nodded.

They waited another ten minutes in silence...

Sam was the first to break it. "Do you think it's still stalking us?"

Jess made a slight grimace. "Hard to tell. It might be."

"Well, we can't exactly stay here all day, can we?"

"No. It will be nightfall soon, and I'd like to be at a traveler's nest by then."

Sam set his jaw and said, "Okay, let's go."

He took half a dozen steps forward before the massive bird of prey flew up from beneath the bridge. It lashed out with its razor-sharp talons.

But before they could connect with Sam, Tom opened fire.

The burst of 9mm parabellums ripped through the bird, killing it instantly.

Sam stepped back and grinned. "Thanks, Tom."

"Any time. That's why you bring me along on these stupid adventures... to save your ass."

"That's true." To Jess, he said, "You want to tell me what the hell that thing was?"

CHAPTER TEN

Jess said, "It's called a Haast's eagle."

Sam sighed. "A what?"

"Haast's eagle. It's an abbreviation of its Latin name, *Hieraaetus moorei,* an otherwise extinct species of eagle that once lived in the South Island of New Zealand, commonly accepted to be the Pouakai of Maori legend."

"Yet the creature has survived here all this time?"

"Among others, yes," Jess agreed. "The species was the largest eagle known to have existed. Its massive size is explained as an evolutionary response to the size of its prey, the flightless moa, the largest of which could weigh upward of five hundred pounds. But where New Zealand's Haast's eagle became extinct around 1200AD after the moa were hunted to extinction by the first Māori, those inside the 8th Continent have been protected, with plenty of food and very little threat."

Sam's eyes narrowed. "Why didn't the local people here kill them?"

"It's easier said than done." Jess continued to head south along the skyway. "You both carry modern weapons and yet it nearly killed you."

"Sure, but the Māori killed the birds with handheld weapons, so what went wrong here?"

She looked at him directly, her lips parting with a wry and impish smile. "You don't miss a thing, do you?"

"No, I miss plenty of things. It's the obvious that I tend to get. So what is it?"

"The truth is, humans decided to let them live."

"Why?"

"Because they keep down the number of marsupial lions that would otherwise strip the region of its human inhabitants."

"So they kept one predator to protect them from another?"

She shrugged. "Like I said, there's a different mindset here. People think and act differently than those on the surface."

Tom said, "That's sure as hell right. If these were surface humans, both Haast's eagle and the marsupial lion would now be extinct."

No more Haast's eagles troubled them on their way to the traveler's nest.

But still, Sam felt like he was being watched. He kept checking over his shoulder and spotted the merest shadow of other humans.

"Someone's out there," Sam said.

Jess shrugged. "Of course there is. There are plenty of travelers who use the skyway."

"So then why haven't we seen any of them?"

"It's a dangerous part of the land. People don't willingly try to reveal their presence to strangers in this part of the 8th Continent..."

In the end, Sam let it go—but still, he felt like he was being watched—and possibly stalked.

The last of the strange purple sun was setting on the horizon by the time they climbed the steep ladder to a massive treehouse, perched on top of an ancient Eucalyptus regnans.

The traveler's nest rivaled the Swiss Family Robinson's treehouse. It was built out of a series of interwoven vines, branches, and a thick thatch roof. Spanning three stories, the nest provided ample sleeping accommodations.

A small forest of vines surrounded the tree house nest, and on these were a plethora of dark red berries.

Jess picked a handful, eating some herself, and handing the others to Sam and Tom. "Have a try, they're full of vitamins and nutrients."

Sam took a bite. It was sour and crunchy. Kind of what he'd expect from a cross between citrus fruit and protein rich nuts. He forced himself to finish it without saying anything.

She laughed. "What do you think?"

"They're a little sour."

"Yeah. Not one of our more delightful treats, but it will provide all the nutrients you need to survive on your journey. They were planted here years ago for weary travelers. There are also water fountains, fed by the river below if you're thirsty."

"Okay, thanks."

Almost as soon as the sun had set, blue bioluminescent birds rose up from the forest, lighting the night sky with a constellation every bit as spectacular as the stars seen from above ground. As the velvet black darkness of night took over, the obsidian grotto turned into a vibrant constellation of blue-green stars. Sam relaxed back into a section of the nest that formed a lounge come bed, and stared up at the myriad of moving incandescent blue birds as they appeared like shooting stars throughout a galaxy of glow worms.

"All right, I know I've said it before, Tom, but now I really have seen it all."

Tom laughed. "Yeah, it's something all right."

Jess glanced at them both. "What?"

"What do you mean, what?" Sam asked, his lips curling

upward into a wry grin. "We're talking about the blue iridescent birds! If I lived here, I could watch them all night."

Jess laughed. "You haven't ever seen blue glowing birds?"

"Ah… no," Sam and Tom replied in unison.

Sam said, "Glow worms, yes. Glow birds… no."

"How very bizarre." Jess leaned back, crossing her legs. "I had never even considered that they're anything unusual."

"Well they are," Sam said, decidedly. "I've never seen anything like it."

"Actually…" Jess said, "I once read a book on ornithology from the surface."

"And?" Sam asked. "You really are a wealth of knowledge."

"Well, it turns out, millions of years ago, all bird feathers had the ability to luminesce under the right conditions, and most had bioluminescent abilities."

"I wonder why the genetic trait died out?" Sam asked, his voice taking on a hint of sarcasm. "It would have been like lighting up a smorgasbord for dinner to the larger predators."

Tom crossed his arms behind his head to form a makeshift pillow and leaned back. "And yet there isn't a problem with them here…"

"I can answer that one," Jess said.

Sam and Tom turned to look at her. "Go on. Why?"

"It has to do with the Haast's eagle. It dominates the sky in the day, and sleeps at night, leaving only nocturnal birds to feed on the glow worms that are abundant on the roof of the 8th Continent at night."

"Interesting," Sam said, crossing his arms. "Now tell me this. How did your grandmother get stuck here?"

Jess turned her head, looking away from him. "Isn't it obvious?"

"No."

"Amelia Earhart, my grandmother, flew here by accident."

Her voice softened, becoming slower and somehow more distant as she spoke. "As you well know, she was on her way to be the first woman to circumnavigate the world as a pilot back in 1937."

Sam nodded. Amelia Earhart had been an inspiration to him for many years. Not because of the mystery surrounding her death, but because of her tenacity and strong will that had allowed her to overcome so many other obstacles to get there in the first place. For him, the fact she was remembered for the way she had died and not how she had lived was the greatest tragedy. "I know about Amelia."

Her voice turned cold, confrontational. "Do you really, Mr. Reilly?"

"I know she didn't grow up rich, as one would have expected a woman must have been to go on to become one of the world's greatest aviators in a time when few men knew how to fly." Sam smiled, still amazed to think that he was talking to the legend's granddaughter. "I know she dropped out of college as soon as World War I started and became a nurse at a military hospital, where she first met aviators and became intrigued by the idea of flight. She was nearly a century ahead of her time. In a period when women were expected to do little else than stay at home, raise babies, keep the house clean, and put food on the table for her husband, she became a pilot. In 1931 she married publicist, George Putnam, retaining her maiden name and demanded the marriage be an equal partnership. I know she was an intelligent, tenacious, adventurer, who wanted to go out and explore the world — because it was there."

Jess's breathing became shallow. She turned her gaze to meet him directly, a small tear forming in her left eye. She exhaled deeply. "I see… so you did know my grandmother."

"She was a remarkable person… and an inspiration to all." Sam took her hand, squeezing it gently. "Can you tell me what happened?"

Jess squeezed his hand and then let it go again. "When a

navigation error led her to land on a small atoll on the Phoenix Islands, she refueled from a secret Japanese fuel cache she discovered, before being attacked—the Japanese patrol killed Amelia's navigator, Fred Noonan, and she was forced to leave him, as she took off. From there, she flew southeast toward New Zealand, but must have overshot the two islands, instead flying onward farther out into the Pacific Ocean. By the time she had discovered her mistake, she was too far east to return to New Zealand. When she ran out of fuel, she landed on a small atoll, the one that you now see positioned under the first obsidian dome at the entrance to the 8th Continent."

Sam said, "But it's nearly fifty feet under water?"

"That's right. Amelia walked down into the same set of obsidian stairs that you used to enter the 8th Continent and discovered a hidden world, filled with fresh water, edible fruits, streams filled with fish, and a native population who were accepting of what few outsiders it received." Jess paused for a minute, regathering what she knew, and considering which parts to tell and which to leave out. "She spent the next few months living here, building a makeshift home, and ensuring that she could survive for the long term. She figured there wasn't much of a rush to return to the surface of the atoll, because if anyone did find her wreckage, they would trace her steps through the obsidian archway, and down below."

"But she did go to the surface. Somewhere along the line, she took her camera—with photos of people long forgotten—and placed it inside the Electra, which is how I found it. So what happened to the atoll?"

Jess smiled. "Indeed. What did happen to Amelia's atoll? The truth is, I still don't know. By the time Amelia returned to the surface, she found the entire place was cocooned in a giant dome of obsidian, like some sort of crazy science experiment. Her entire world had become submerged."

"How long did she live?"

"It was a long time ago… I don't really know." Jess said the words quickly, like someone slamming a book shut.

"And your parents?"

"They're both gone, too."

Sam frowned. "I'm sorry. Really, I am. No wonder you didn't want to talk about it."

"It's all right." Jess spoke softly. "I was happy to tell the story. Come on, we should get some sleep, we have a lot of ground to cover tomorrow before we reach the maze."

CHAPTER ELEVEN

The Maze, 8th Continent

THE NEXT MORNING SAM AWOKE to the dark purple light of predawn, as it broke the velvet night's sky. All three of them rose quickly, having a quick meal of berries and a drink of ice-cold water, before continuing south along the skyway.

They moved from tree to tree with a series of military style tactical maneuvers designed to protect each other from another attack by Haast's eagles. Sam made the first sprint across the bridge, being covered by Tom, and then he would cover Tom as he crossed, and they would both cover Jess as she made the sprint.

It was a slow process, but it was the only way to be certain they would reach their destination as a party of three.

By midday they climbed a higher section of the skyway and stopped. To the east of the river, they were presented with a giant panorama of a new landscape, one that took Sam's breath away. Unlike the undulating, semi-mountainous region through which they had been traveling for the past two days, he now looked upon the great plains of the 8th Continent.

His eyes traced the new landscape with awe.

There were a series of interwoven, straight waterways feeding out from the Sentinel River. A labyrinth of aqueducts and irrigation, leading east until they reached the maze — miles upon miles of convoluted pathways, tunnels and bridges built out of a combination of obsidian and thick leafy vegetation.

"There's the maze," Jess said.

Sam took out a pair of binoculars and studied the maze. He clicked the shutter button, and it took a digital photo, which he brought up on his computer tablet. There he studied the maze, mapping out the most direct route, and up to five circuitous routes, mapping each one separately.

Sam set his jaw firm. "It doesn't look very complicated."

Jess smiled. "Yeah, well... looks can be deceiving..."

He picked up his binoculars again, and fixed them directly at the large open space at the center of the maze. The prize for navigating the strange region and overcoming the challenges.

The center of the maze was covered in verdant green grass, with cattle and sheep casually dotted around, grazing peacefully. A massive colonial-style sandstone building stood proudly to the east, overlooking the estate. It reminded him of a castle overlooking its English countryside. Beside the building stood a smaller one, possibly a set of stables, and a barn for farm animals. A single stream ran from the north to the south of the land, with a single waterwheel feeding its agriculture, and a large opaline lake adorning the center of the paradise.

Sam put his binoculars away. "So, how do we get down?"

"That's the easy part," Jess said. "Come with me."

Sam said, "Easy; that's what I like to hear."

Jess brought them to a small platform on the side of the viewing tower. A thick rope supported the platform via a pulley system constructed high above on top of a large tripod.

"There's a second platform on the ground currently," she

said, pointing to the ground far below. "This is a counter-weighted elevator. Basically, the two platforms have hollow piping which can be filled with water through a plumbing point here."

Tom examined the mechanism, his face set with incredulity. "Why did the Master Builders design such a complex system?"

She arched an eyebrow. "Why not a rope to simply slide down?"

"Yeah," Tom said. "That would have been simpler."

"Because, the skyway is used for travelers and merchants. Even though food is far from scarce, resources are, and there are traveling merchants who shift valuable resources using the skyway. They need a large enough system to raise their goods."

"All right, sounds better than that harrowing climb at the other end of the skyway." Sam stepped onto the platform. "So how do we do this?"

Jess stepped next to him. "Everyone on board. Hold on."

She waited until Tom shuffled on board, and then adjusted a control in the middle which looked like a gear stick, turning it to open. "The platform at the bottom is currently full of water. Its counterweight is keeping us held firm up here. Right now, I'm emptying some of that water. When it becomes lighter than us, we will start heading toward the ground."

Sam said, "Not too fast I hope!"

"No, not unless I shift this pump all the way to the right."

Jess pretended to move the stick, but Sam stopped her. "No… slow is fine!"

The counterweight elevator creaked and a minute later it started to descend.

At the bottom, Sam stared up at the giant trees above. The place looked like something out of Peter Pan's Neverland.

Sam checked his compass, matching it to a southeastern direction to set a course for the entrance to the maze. Before he was finished, Jess had already started moving in that direction, with the confidence of someone who'd made the journey many times before.

They walked past the series of labyrinthine waterways that crisscrossed out from the river to irrigate a series of natural fields.

Jess said, "You might want to keep your weapons out. It can be a little dangerous out here, while we're still near the Sentinel River, but it will get safer as we get closer to the maze."

Sam gripped his MP5, scanning the short grass nearby for signs of any living creature. There wasn't much and nothing big enough to cause them any harm. "What exactly should we be keeping our eyes out for?"

"You'll know when it comes for you," Jess said without altering her stride. "Just keep moving."

"Great..." Tom said, "We'll just ah... keep our eyes out for anything that's going to try and kill us."

"That's a good motto here in the 8th Continent," Jess said cheerfully.

They reached the entrance to the maze by early afternoon.

It was a single arched opening in the middle of a solid wall of obsidian, some thirty feet high. It seemed more intimidating up close.

Sam stopped and had a quick drink from his water bottle. He glanced inside. The entrance led to a single passageway that ran at least a hundred feet inward. Removing his tablet, he checked the image in his program. It matched up precisely, putting an image of an old Pacman creature where they were on the map and an X at the center of the maze.

Jess urged them on. "We need to move quickly. There's only about four hours of sunlight left. We need to make sure we're out of the maze before dark, or we'll never get out."

Sam's lips curled into a wry smile. "Why?"

Jess said, "Because I don't plan on spending eternity inside some stupid maze."

"No, I mean, I have an aerial digital photo of the maze on my tablet, with the most direct route programmed into it. I realize you've never used GPS, but this program will basically map out any intricate detail, so that we know precisely where we are at any time. So, I think you'll discover we'll be able to find our way through quickly in the dark or the light."

She laughed. "Not this maze."

Sam adjusted the straps to his backpack, slinging his weapon over his shoulder and keeping his tablet out.

Jess shook her head. "You might find you'll want to swap that tablet for something more useful."

Sam held his tablet up. "This will be useful. Just wait and see."

"No. It won't. And definitely not as useful as that pop-gun you keep on carrying."

Sam said, "I can reach it quick as I need. Besides, Tom's a better shot than I am."

"You'd better hope so."

They entered the maze, walking approximately forty feet inside before they heard it.

Sam stopped. The noise was quiet and distant, but none-the-less clearly distinguishable — it was the echo of an animal's growl.

His eyes scanned the open passageway up ahead. It was gun barrel straight and empty. The maze was made up of vertical and horizontal passageways. Whatever was coming for them, they still had time. Besides, an animal wasn't going to get far against their weapons.

He turned to Jess. "You never mentioned how the maze prevents all predators from entering…"

"That's right."

The growl came louder now, echoing through the maze.

Sam said, "How exactly does the maze do that?"

The lines around Jess's face deepened. "Didn't I mention… the maze is home to a pride of marsupial lions."

Sam said, "You might have neglected to mention that."

Tom aimed his weapon down the passageway.

Sam said, "We're only forty odd feet from the exit. We should leave and you can fill us in with everything we need to know about marsupial lions before we start."

Jess sighed. "I'm afraid it's too late for that. We can't get out now. The only way out is to go through the maze."

Sam said, "What are you talking about? The exit it right behind us!"

"No, it isn't."

Sam felt a lump in his throat as he turned to face the exit, which was now a solid wall of obsidian. He grabbed his computer tablet, his eyes landing on the map. It now showed simply a question mark over the entire maze.

Sam turned on Jess, "What the hell's going on?"

Jess swallowed. "Oh, by the way… the maze is alive."

CHAPTER TWELVE

J ESS SAW DOUBT AND FEAR fixed on Sam Reilly's face.

But there was a hardened resolve there, too. With the quick movements of a seasoned soldier, Sam had his weapon already out, loaded with a full magazine. His jaw was set firm, and his intelligent ocean blue eyes filled with the poise and acuity of a man used to being in charge of any situation. Next to him, Tom wore a bemused smile of indifference—as though being trapped in a moving, living, maze was nothing particularly out of the ordinary.

Sam said, "All right, Jess. Your move. Now what?"

She met his eye. "Now, you'd better follow me exactly, or we'll all be killed. How does that work for you?"

"Suits me," Sam said.

"Good." She turned to Tom. "What about you?"

"I'm just along for the ride and to keep Sam from doing something really stupid," Tom replied, without lowering his weapon. "You sound like you know where you're going. So, we'll just follow you."

Sam said, "But whatever we do, we should do it now."

Jess folded her arms across her chest. "Actually, we have to wait right here."

Sam kept his MP5 aimed down the long passageway. "We're going to wait for them to come to us?"

Jess nodded. "Marsupial lions were once the largest marsupial carnivores anywhere in the world. Despite their name, they're more closely related to diprotodons than lions. They weigh about 250 to 300 pounds with extremely robust, powerfully built jaws and very strong forelimbs. They possess retractable claws, a unique trait among marsupials, allowing them to keep their claws razor sharp while regularly running on hard surfaces—such as obsidian."

The sound of growling was now superimposed with the beat of powerful hind paws racing along the narrow passageways up ahead.

Jess felt her chest tighten. Despite being through this challenge previously, the sound always got to her. She felt her throat try to close up and her breathing becoming labored. She swallowed down the fear and stood her ground.

She spoke in a slow, monotone voice. "They have semi-opposable first digits, like thumbs, with an enlarged claw well suited for climbing trees and grappling with its prey, slicing right through it. They are slower than most predators, better suited for stalking and short bursts—but make no mistake about it, they will kill you if they're allowed to come within reach of you."

"Will our shots kill it?" Tom asked, casually.

"To be honest, I don't know." Jess closed her eyes, concentrating on the sound of the oncoming beasts, rather than their sight. "It doesn't really matter. There are too many for you to kill them all."

Sam shouted, "They're here!"

Jess opened her eyes.

The pride of marsupial lions raced straight at them.

Jess consciously breathed in through her nose. "Whatever you do, don't make a move."

The pride consisted of twenty marsupial lions. The maze was their home. Their territory. And they would protect it from all intruders with their lives.

"Wait for it!" she instructed.

A moment later the pack of beasts disappeared.

In their place was a solid wall of obsidian.

Sam grinned. "What just happened?"

"They triggered one of the passages many turnpikes by stepping on a mechanical paver that's been fixed like a boobytrap," Jess explained. "They now have to run a giant loop to get back to the side we're on. Come on, we don't have a lot of time."

They started to jog down the new horizontal passageway.

Tom said, "If you knew about the turnpike, why didn't we just trigger it and save ourselves the whole deadly predator confrontation?"

"If we had, then we would have opened up the door directly to the lions." Jess breathed heavily as she jogged. "Now, they're the ones racing back to catch us."

They kept moving at a pace just faster than a jog. Sam and Tom had tried to sprint at first, but she encouraged them to slow down. They had a long way to go and would need to conserve their energy in case she made a mistake and they ran into the pride of marsupial lions again.

The passages continued in a unicursal process, more like a labyrinth, folding back on themselves at each end, without appearing to branch out like the traditional multicursal path seen in the maze from above.

She had made this run multiple times before and knew how the maze behaved. Although it wasn't actually alive, it felt very much so. A series of underground aqueducts acted like hydraulics on the maze's some four hundred turnpikes, making it change shape constantly. But what appeared like a series of random unexplained links between passages, had an underlying purpose. Like a Rubik's Cube, a series of algorithms could be used to achieve the desired goal of matching up the colors on the puzzle no matter their position on the cube. In this case, the pieces of the maze kept rotating, but following a well-worn process, she would eventually beat each layer of the maze until she reached the center.

The maze was made up of nine layers, with each one consisting of vertical and horizontal passages. She had reached the eighth one. It was hard to tell how much farther she had to go until the next turnpike. The obsidian walls all looked the same. To make matters worse, the echo of angry predators was a constant, no matter where they were, making it impossible to tell how close they were to the threat.

She turned a corner, and came face to face with the pack of beasts running full speed toward her. Jess turned and yelled, "Other way!"

They raced back the way they had come, using whatever energy they had left to sprint. When the lions reached the turnpike some of them disappeared, but a few moments later, the turnpike spun again, and two lions were left.

My God! They've finally worked out how to play this game.

She yelled, "Run faster!"

CHAPTER THIRTEEN

THE NEXT TURNPIKE WAS TAKING too long to move.

Sam leveled the MP5 at the marsupial lion and squeezed the trigger. The turnpike spun round and they were on the ninth layer of the maze.

Jess said, "Go right!"

Behind them, he heard the sound of many paws sprinting across the cold obsidian floors. It made the three of them run harder, but they could never outrun the ancient predators.

The internal wall was different from the rest of the maze, which looked like identical, smooth, and glassy obsidian. Instead, this one had multiple petroglyphs etched into the obsidian. There were images of pyramids, sarcophagi, looking glass pedestals, labyrinths, and star constellations. There was a wealth of information there, but he didn't dare give any of them more than a passing glance.

He noticed that Jess did though.

She was obviously searching for something in particular, an image that meant something, like a code or a marker for a secret passage.

Jess stopped. "Found it!"

Sam's eyes darted to the wall.

There was a petroglyph of a maze stretching from the floor up to roughly five feet. It could have been the same one they had just navigated, or it could have been completely different. Whatever it was meant to represent, Jess had dedicated all her attention to it.

There were a series of turnpikes hidden in the maze in the form of a raised stone. Jess quickly searched for and depressed each of the stones.

And the marsupial lions ran toward them at full speed.

Sam and Tom each took aim at the beasts to the front of the pride, and fired multiple short bursts, strategically placed to slow the group of predators, more than kill them.

Sam chambered another magazine and continued firing, but the shots had little effect on the oncoming predators.

"Jess!" He shouted. "We're almost out of time!"

"I'm in!"

A small section of the wall, just big enough for them to crawl through, opened inward.

They slipped through, quickly closing the ancient obsidian door behind them.

Its latches had almost locked when a marsupial lion's powerful fore limb protruded, gripping Jess on her right arm. Its razor sharp semi-opposable claw latched onto the arm like a vice, pulling her in toward the obsidian wall.

Tom threw his weight against the door. The beast gnarled as its fore limb became jammed against the obsidian, but its grip on Jess only tightened.

She cried out in pain.

Sam placed the barrel of his Heckler and Koch MP5 submachinegun hard up against the marsupial lion's fore limb and squeezed the trigger—sending a continuous burst of 9mm parabellums into the animal's fore limb, ripping straight through it.

Tom shoved his own 250 pounds of muscle into the ancient obsidian door, and its latches locked.

Sam turned to Jess, whose mauled arm was bleeding badly. "Are you all right?"

She looked down, her face registering surprise at the damage, and said, "I think I need help."

CHAPTER FOURTEEN

THE PAIN SHOT THROUGH HER right arm like lightning.

Jess gripped the wound near her elbow with her left hand, but blood kept on oozing out through her fingers.

Next to her, Sam had dropped his backpack. He opened up the zipper and quickly removed a military tourniquet.

"Lie still!" Sam commanded, as he slid the mechanical tourniquet over her right upper arm. "It's nicked your brachial artery. This is probably going to hurt a little."

"What… more than being mauled by a…" Jess screamed.

And Sam started to twist the mechanical tightening screw.

The blood stopped flowing. She released the pressure from her left hand, examining the wound with detached interest and curiosity. Her eyes turned to Sam and Tom. "Thank you. Both of you for saving my life."

Tom shrugged. "Hey, don't thank me too much. There was plenty of self-interest in trying to keep that door shut."

Her impish smile returned. "All the same. Thank you both."

Sam asked, "Are we safe here?"

She nodded, "Yes. We've reached the center of the maze. A land of total safety, built by the Master Builders, as a place for them to come together."

"There are multiple Master Builders here?"

"Sometimes."

She went to stand up, but Sam placed a hand on her shoulder to stop her.

"Not yet. You'll lose your arm if I leave that tourniquet on it."

Her eyes narrowed. "So what are you proposing?"

"We have a suture kit in the bag."

"You're a trained doctor?"

Sam said, "No. But my aunt insisted I learn to sew as a kid. It's basically the same thing. You'll probably have a scar, but it will be better than losing an arm. What do you think?"

"Sure. Why not?"

It took Sam roughly ten to fifteen minutes to place three sutures in the wound on her arm. He wrapped the outside of the wound with a saline soaked gauze, and then bandaged it. When he was finished, he slowly loosened the tourniquet.

She examined his handy work. No blood leaked through the dressing. "Hey, you're not bad at this."

Sam smiled. "Thanks."

Jess gripped his hand appreciatively and pulled herself up onto her feet. She felt dizzy for a moment, but quickly regained her balance. "Do you want to meet the Master Builders?"

CHAPTER FIFTEEN

A BORDER COLLIE RAN UP to meet them. Sam leaned down to pat the sheep dog, which responded to the attention with its tail wagging cheerfully. They walked across the acres of verdant grass to the palatial homestead.

A man approached them from the stables. He was tall and wore a blue uniform that reminded Sam of the decorative dress uniforms of some sort of medieval army, yet the man appeared to carry no weapon. He looked no different than any other modern human.

"Hello," the man said looking at Jess. "You look like you had a bit of trouble with the maze today. That was careless of you."

Jess embraced the man with a warm hug. "I very nearly got myself killed."

"Like I said, awfully careless." The man looked up at Sam and Tom, as though only just now realizing the presence of two strangers. "I'm sorry, I'm the Caretaker."

"Sam," he said, offering his hand. "And this is Tom."

The man took it with a firm and leathery grip. "Pleasure.

Welcome. We don't get a lot of visitors here, as you can imagine. Which reminds me, why are you here?"

Jess said, "They've come to meet the Gifted Ones."

The Caretaker frowned. "Then I'm afraid they might be a little disappointed."

Sam held his breath. "Why?"

"The Gifted Ones have gone to the topside for a while."

"Any idea when they will be back?"

"It's hard to say. Sometimes they go for days, but if they leave the 8th Continent they can be gone for months."

"Great. Then we've come a long way for nothing."

Jess said, "Not nothing. Come inside. There's a map I'd like to show you."

Sam and Tom followed her inside the main sandstone building, while the Caretaker continued on with his work tending to the horses in the stables.

The interior of the colonial style house looked like it had been ripped out of the 18th century gentry. There was rich royal blue carpet, a mahogany staircase, even an old gramophone. Jess put on an old record, and some classical music, which he didn't recognize, started to play.

She took them to a large billiards room.

Sam struggled to imagine a bunch of Master Builders drinking beer and playing billiards. He dismissed the thought from his mind as his eyes locked on a large map, presumably of the 8th Continent, mounted on the wall.

Jess smiled. "Well, what do you think?"

Sam shook his head as he examined the map. "It's amazing."

There were four distinctively different quadrants, representing each of the seasons, as Jess had described. He looked at the northeast quadrant, where the maze was depicted in full. His eyes traced the Sentinel River as it ran due south, splitting the continent in two. Unable to head east due to the freezing environment, the river meandered to the west to form a definite distinction from the desert of permanent summer, and then ran north again, through fall, before being released at the two hundred foot waterfall he'd seen at the entrance to the spring quadrant.

He focused in on the manmade structures in the inhospitable southern quadrants. His eyes narrowed and he felt his heart pound in his chest. There, near the peak of the snow covered mountain was the image of a pyramid. Any doubt he had that the Gifted Ones were indeed Master Builders was suddenly removed.

Tom, feigning disinterest, casually set up the billiard table and started to play.

"Have you ever been here?" Sam asked, pointing to the pyramid.

"No. I've never been to the southern quadrants." She smiled. "But I've seen the one in the spring quadrant."

Sam raised an eyebrow. "There's more than one pyramid?"

"Yes, there are four in total."

He turned his attention to the lava filled land at the farthest southwest section of the map. There, in the middle of what appeared to be a permanent sea of lava from an active volcano was another golden pyramid.

Sam met her eye. "Any idea how someone goes about traveling to a land filled with lava?"

"I don't know..." she laughed. "I suppose you would want to wear some sort of protective suit. Although why you'd want to go there, I don't know."

"What about the pyramid in the northeast?" he asked, staring at the pyramid that was depicted in the middle of the region most densely populated by Homo sapiens.

"What about it?" she asked.

"Have you been inside?"

"No. There are no doors. Only giant stones that appear

golden in the sun. I'm told the Gifted Ones can enter."

"One day, I would like to come back here for a much longer time, and see what I can learn from these pyramids—and ideally, what I can do to help the Master Builders." His tone turned serious. "The real question, though, is what do we do about the 8th Continent?"

Jess met his question with hostility. "What do you mean, do?"

"I mean, this place has remained hidden from the world for millennia. What about the human inhabitants? You said that they've evolved differently because they have ample resources in terms of food and shelter, but little others to promote scientific advancement, such as metals, and fuel sources. When I return to my government, what should I say?"

"You mean, should the discovery of the 8th Continent be passed onto the rest of the world?"

"Exactly…" Sam said. "What do you think?"

"I think we're living in utopia. The last Garden of Eden on Earth."

Sam asked, "You don't want anything to change?"

"It's not up to me."

"Who is it up to then?"

"There will need to be a gathering of the elders. There will be a vote. But I have an idea I know what they will say."

Sam looked at her gray eyes. "And what's that?"

"They will want independence."

"That might be hard to enforce when the location of the 8th Continent comes out."

She shook her head. "We can defend ourselves. If need be, we can destroy the entrance, and no one from the surface will ever see this world again."

Sam sighed heavily, acknowledging the threat. "I'll do my best to help."

"Just give us enough time to make a decision. When we do,

I'll contact you and let you know what we've decided."

"You can contact me?"

She smiled. "If you leave me your phone number, I can. The Gifted Ones have a phone with a direct line to the outside world, here."

"Okay. We'll head home in the morning and I'll await your call."

"I need to stay here for a few more days," she said. "Do you think you can find the entrance on your own?"

"Sure I can…" Sam grinned. "Well, so long as Tom helps me."

CHAPTER SIXTEEN

═══════⧚⊰⟨✕⟩⊱⧛═══════

SHE WATCHED SAM AND TOM leave the maze.

The Caretaker approached, his jaw set firm and his steely gaze leveled at her. "You were supposed to kill them... what happened?"

"I liked them."

"What difference does it make whether or not you liked them? They're going to come back here with an army. We've just started a war on the Master Builders. Don't you think it's a little dangerous to release their allies back to the surface? You've seen their weapons; we'll be no match against them."

"No they won't. That wasn't what they came for."

"What are you talking about? Why else would the Gifted Ones have sent for them?"

"The Gifted Ones didn't send for them. They came looking for the truth about Amelia Earhart."

"Seriously?"

"Yeah."

"All right. But it's only a matter of time before they realize the truth about this place… people will flock from all around the world to come here."

"I know."

"What did you tell them?"

"That I would discuss it with the council, but we would be looking for our independence."

The Caretaker's eyes narrowed. "You think that was wise?"

She met his gaze with defiance. "It's time we start developing our own allies from the outside."

The Caretaker nodded. "You're certain you can trust him?"

"Yes."

"All right. Let's see where this takes us." The man paused, taking it all in. "Did you tell him the truth about your past?"

She shook her head. "No. It would be too much. It would change the negotiations completely. Then we really would have the world coming down here, searching for the one resource more valuable than gold."

The Caretaker squeezed her hand. "You made the right choice, Amelia."

CHAPTER SEVENTEEN

Sea Gypsy Gathering, Mergui Archipelago

THE MOKEN PEOPLE, WHO LIVE in the Mergui Archipelago—some eight hundred tiny islands scattered across nearly three hundred miles of Andaman Sea off the coast of Thailand and Myanmar—have lived as nomadic seafarers for more than four thousand years, since their migration from southern China in 2000 BC.

The ancient hunter gatherers spend nearly their entire lives out at sea, living on small wooden hand dugout boats called kabangs, only ever coming to shore to make repairs and to gather sea shells for cooking, pandanus leaves for their sails, or to take refuge from the most severe monsoon. Throughout the course of the year, they tie their boats together to form a flotilla—a living community out at sea to which dozens of families may belong.

The only possessions they desire are their boats and a few simple seafood-gathering tools. They share everything they have, even with strangers, a custom based on the belief that the sea is bountiful and there is enough for all. They show virtually no signs of materialism or greed. They don't save; they don't want possessions because carrying a lot of things only slows them down. They catch only what they need for the day and never use nets. They don't try to make large catches and never sell what they've caught. Any excess is shared with family, friends, strangers, and their community. Individuals are happy if their community is doing well and sad when their community struggles.

This type of egalitarian lifestyle has led to the interesting development of their unique Moken language, which doesn't have any Moken equivalent for common Western words such as, *when, take, worry, want, hello,* or *goodbye.*

Katale smiled, his big white teeth shining bright against the backdrop of his dark, suntanned skin. His eyes were large, and doe-like, giving him a more youthful appearance, despite his lean and muscular body. At twelve years of age, he was still little more than a boy, but he fished like a man, and could dive better than those many years older than him.

The fishing had been poor today.

Something had gotten the fish spooked. It happened. Sometimes it indicated a sudden change in weather, a great storm was coming, or that there had been a submarine earthquake. Sometimes it portended a great disaster, like in 2004 when the great sea spirit came to the shore of the islands and ate thousands of people. Katale wasn't alive then, but he'd heard about the story, about how his people had known of the upcoming disaster and warned many people, saving many lives throughout the archipelago.

It didn't feel like any of that today.

There was something else entirely different happening. There was a disturbance in the sea and things were about to change forever.

And that made him happy.

Because he wasn't the only one who would be curious.

The crayfish would have sensed the change as well as he did, and they had left the safety of the reef.

And that's why he was smiling. Because he would find the biggest one and bring it back to his father. Tonight, their family would feast on crayfish.

He sailed his kabang at a fast pace, riding a gentle, but firm, southerly wind.

Katale was proud of his kabang.

Boat building was a skill passed down through the generations from father to son. This was his second one, and by far the best in the Andaman Sea. It was carved hollow from a single, old-growth log, then hauled to the beach, where the hull and roof were painstakingly built during the last monsoon season.

It had taken him nearly four months to build.

His boat was traditional. It was painted black and had curved notches in the bow and stern to symbolize a mouth and an anus, representing that the ship is a living, breathing entity that eats the sea. Most modern kabang had motors. But his father didn't believe in them, instead, recommending that he should power the ship with traditional oars and sails made of pandanus leaves. Being lighter than those with slow diesel motors, his kabang could move nearly a full two knots faster than those which had succumbed to some of the more modern technologies.

Running with the wind was like sailing in a dream. His large single square sail, made of woven pandanus, was fully open. Because the boat was being drawn by the movement of the air, it felt calming, with the sensation of very little wind — yet there was plenty of movement.

He reached the outer reef by the time the sun was two-thirds of its way through its cycle overhead. Katale furled the single sail, and dropped an anchor made of a large stone tied to rope.

Katale didn't wait to check that his kabang was secure. He

instinctively knew that the anchor had bitten the sand below. He took a couple deep breaths and dived off the boat, into the turquoise waters.

The lives of the Moken people have been entwined with the sea for so many years that they have become amphibious creatures, as comfortable in the sea as they were out of the water. Their children learned to swim before they ever learned to walk. Their eyes could see twice as well underwater as their Western counterparts, allowing them to focus on and pick out small shellfish and other sea life from the rocky ocean floor that would otherwise be just a blur. The human eye was adapted to function optimally in air and its focusing capability deteriorates underwater. That's why we need goggles to see clearly while swimming, but Moken children are able to constrict their pupils, thereby producing sharper images.

At twelve years of age, Katale was probably the best free diver from his flotilla.

He opened his eyes and swam deep into the crystal-clear waters. He swallowed to equalize the pressure in his ears and dived quickly. At forty feet, he reached the bottom of the outer reef, where the crayfish could normally be found. He ducked down, so that he could see beneath the shallow overhanging reef.

Nothing.

No fish swimming and no crayfish hiding.

He turned, and kept swimming along the bottom of the reef, his eyes constantly scanning for signs of sea life.

Nearly two minutes went by and he turned to make his way to the surface for air.

But something stopped him.

Out the corner of his eyes, he spotted something. It was in the sandy seabed another twenty feet deeper, and it was flickering in response to the rays of the sun. It looked like the gold the visitors to the islands from lands far away used to wear. The stuff they seemed to covet more than any other material. He didn't care for its appearance, but he knew the value of gold. It could be used to entice fish, making it a great fishing tool.

His curiosity piqued, Katale swam deeper toward the seabed.

As he got closer, the light disappeared.

He paused, mid-stroke, his eyes fixing on it again.

It flickered again.

It was gold!

He swam faster.

By now his lungs were burning, but he had to know the truth. He had to see it. The fear of losing whatever it was, was too much for him.

Again, the light stopped. He ran his hands through the sandy seabed. Something just below the surface appeared smooth, like glass.

He dug at the sand, pulling with both hands. There was definitely something there below it. Something smooth.

He cleared away a small layer of sand, revealing a large glassy surface, in the shape of a dome. He could see it clearly now. The object was made of glass. It was too large for him to reach either side of it, making it more like the size of a boat than a piece of jewelry. It looked like it had been buried there years ago. When and for what purpose he had no idea. He placed his eye right up to the glass, as though he could somehow see what was inside.

Katale stared at the strange sphere.

Could it have been an old sea creature, like the remains of an ancient abalone shell left discarded by the evil sea spirits? His face was pressed close to the sphere. A light originating from the sphere flashed and the inside suddenly became visible.

There, an old man, with white hair, stared back at him.

He was carrying a metallic canister. It had a strange emblem that Katale had never seen before, painted on the side.

If Katale had any air left to exhale, he would have screamed. Instead he froze.

Inside, the man placed a single finger up to his lips — *Shush.*

CHAPTER EIGHTEEN

KATALE WAS THE LAST ONE back to the flotilla. He met his father, who informed him that something strange was happening with the sea, and no one had caught any fish today. Their mood was not somber. The sea would provide for them again tomorrow. The Moken worshipped two spirit gods—the good and the evil. Shamanism was the central element during the spirit festival.

Tonight, they made an additional devotional offering to the two spirit gods.

Afterward, Katale sat with his father and told him all about what he'd seen below the sand of the outer reef. His father didn't really believe him. After all, for what purpose could the good and evil spirits have for a world beneath the sea? But he agreed to see it in the morning.

The next morning they returned to the same site.

Katale dived down to the same place. There were no markings, but there didn't need to be. He knew the outer reef better than any other person alive.

Yet he found nothing.

He dug in the sand, pulling big clumps of sand out, like a kid digging a hole at the beach, but the void inside revealed nothing of yesterday's discovery.

On the surface, his father said, "Are you sure you didn't dream it?"

"I'm certain, father. I swam here yesterday and there was a clear, curved device, like the windows you see on the Thai fishing ships. I could see through it clearly, and on the other side was an old man, with white hair. It's there, I'm sure of it."

"You just dug, and found nothing?" his father countered.

"Maybe they moved it?"

"No," his dad replied, "If it's as big as you say it was, there's no way they could have dug it up and brought it to the surface so fast. You're certain you have the right place?"

Katale nodded. "Yes. It's only a few feet from a cave where I collect crayfish regularly."

His father sighed and then took a deep breath. "Then we'd better keep digging."

Katale and his father made three more trips down to the same spot on the seabed. Each time they shifted more and more sand, and each time, his father became more and more skeptical.

But on the fourth time he shifted a handful of sand and his fingers brushed up against something smooth, like glass.

His father saw it flicker, and quickly started to help remove more sand.

It took an hour for the two of them to clear away an area nearly five feet wide, but all it revealed was more of the strange dome shape.

His father said, "We need to collect fish or we will be hungry tonight. Tomorrow I will come back here with a gathering of the sea gypsies, and we'll find out what this place really is."

Katale spent the rest of that day fishing. He found some of the fish had returned, but not in their previously vast numbers. He caught a few, and returned to the main flotilla. His father was still out gathering a group of sea gypsies—he would not come home for a couple days—and by then all would be explained.

A couple days came and went and Katale didn't see his father.

On the third day, his mother came to him.

She asked, "Have you seen your father in your travels?"

"No. He was out gathering a meeting of the sea gypsies. He might not be home for days. Why? Is something wrong?"

She shook her head. "He never reached any of the sea gypsies."

Katale raised an incredulous eyebrow. "None of them?"

"No. I've asked around. No one has seen him."

"That's strange," Katale admitted.

"He will be all right," his mother said, emphatically. "He is wise and the spirit gods like him."

He nodded in agreement. To him, his father was bigger than anyone he'd ever met—mentally as well as physically—he was a giant of a man.

Katale looked up from their flotilla.

A large iron ship, bigger than anything he'd ever seen in his life, was moving slowly across the turquoise waters of the Mergui Archipelago.

He grinned at the sight of it. "What is that?"

His mother shook her head. "I don't know. It's been here for the past few days. They're saying it's a navy battleship from some place far away."

"Where?"

"The others don't know where it is, but someone said the name is, Russia."

"Russia?" Katale tried the name out. "I've never heard of it before…"

CHAPTER NINETEEN

US Naval Base, San Diego, California

SAM REILLY FELT HIS HEART beat faster at the sight of her. Next to him, his entire crew stood beaming with pride and pleasure, mixed in with a sense of loss for their older and reliable workhorse, the *Maria Helena*. It had taken just six months to design and construct the replacement ship. An extraordinary accomplishment, only capable of being achieved because of the hard work of a massive team of naval and aeronautical engineers from the US Department of Defense, along with civilian contractors, and some of the brightest minds in the industry.

The ship was designed at the US Navy's advanced technologies lab in Quonset, New York, to Sam Reilly's specifications, before having her composite hull put together at the Naval shipyards in San Diego. The ship was to be a replacement for the *Maria Helena,* which had been destroyed by torpedoes during a recovery mission for the *USS Omega Deep,* the US Navy's most advanced experimental submarine. The

Omega Deep had been stolen. As a reward for recovering the Navy's 30-billion-dollar piece of military hardware, the Chief of the US Navy offered to foot the bill for the *Maria Helena's* replacement.

The new ship was slowly pulled into view along a set of purpose-built rails by a pair of Peterbilt trucks. She was an awesome machine—a unique combination of beauty, raw power, and seafaring capabilities. She had a length of 180 feet and a beam of 45 feet. Shaped like a bullet, with a long black hull and narrow beam tapering in to a razor-sharp bow, she looked like one in the water, too.

The command center was positioned amidships, and all below deck, making her comfortable to control in any weather. The hull was made from high tensile and high strength composite materials, and incorporated the same camouflaging technology employed on the *USS Omega Deep,* making the hull capable of becoming translucent from the inside out.

The entire system was autonomous, with the capability of being manually controlled with a wheel from the skipper's chair. The command center even had the feel of a submarine, with stations for the entire crew within close proximity, including an array of sonar, radar, bathymetric, and other high-tech oceanography equipment, satellite communications and navigation, weather station, and a not so small array of hidden weaponry and counter weapons, in the event this vessel was ever met by a similar attack.

Behind the command center was a large rooftop helipad, which could be retracted during rough seas via an internal elevator, allowing the helicopter to be housed internally within the hull, while also making room for a second helicopter to land if need be. The aft deck was flat, and capable of towing large vessels.

Below decks, an internal dive room housed two Atmospheric Dive Suits designed specifically to Sam and Tom's body shapes, a new Triton 36,000/3 submarine, and multiple dive lockers with SCUBA equipment for all of the crew. Unlike the *Maria Helena*, she didn't boast a moonpool that could rival something from an old James Bond film. Instead, the submarine could be launched via a large mechanical lockout locker in the keel. Alternatively, the forward keel used a small lockout locker, similar to those used on nuclear submarines, from which the Atmospheric Dive Suits, SCUBA divers, or ROV remote operated underwater vehicles could be deployed.

She was powered by twin Rolls Royce 28,000hp MTU diesel engines, and twin ZF gearboxes that projected the force of the combined 56,000 hp into four HT1000 HamiltonJet waterjets. Marrying this power to her unique hull shape, she was able to lift out of the water onto the aquaplane at speeds of 60 knots — making her the fastest motor yacht of her size in the world.

A unique system of hydraulic manipulators, allowed the exterior hull shape to be constantly autonomously changed in order to meet the sea conditions. In calm waters, it would force water outward, leaving only a narrow section of the hull to skim across the surface as it aquaplaned. In turbulent seas, the same system could be reversed, digging more of the hull beneath the water, riding very low and safe in the waves.

Across her gunmetal gray hull was the ship's name–

Tahila

The secretary of defense stood quietly in her dress suit. She was tall, with short-cropped, dark red hair and intelligent emerald green eyes, which registered displeasure.

"Good God!" she said, turning to face Sam directly. With her jaw set firm, she took a deep breath. It was a practiced state of serenity, without which she probably would have resigned her position years ago. "Mr. Reilly, when I said the Department of Defense would foot the bill for your replacement ship, I didn't expect you to take advantage of the offer by building something like this. No wonder Defense ran over budget."

Sam frowned. "I'm very sorry, Madam Secretary."

She sighed. "It's all right. I'll make sure the government that paid for it gets the most value out of your use of it."

"Yes, ma'am. I wouldn't have it any other way."

The Commander of the Navy, John Alsop, a sixty-two year old man in his full military dress uniform, approached. "Madam Secretary. We're ready to begin."

"Very good, Commander."

She turned to Sam. "Mark my words. I will see that you pay for every penny we've spent on this ship, in service to your country."

Sam suppressed his smirk. "Yes, ma'am. Understood."

With that, she turned and followed the Commander to take part in the launching ceremony.

Sam watched with pleasure as the Secretary of Defense gave a short speech before striking a bottle of 2008 vintage, Dom Pérignon Rosé on the hull for good luck. A moment later, the Commander nodded his head, and a Petty Officer removed the slipway's lock.

A moment later, the *Tahila* began its sideways journey down the slipway before landing in San Diego Bay — sending an eight-foot wave racing across the bay.

Three hours later, Sam and his crew had run through a series of safety checks on the vessel, and Matthew Sutherland — his skipper — officially took command of the ship. As part of the official launch, Sam, Tom, Genevieve, Elise, Veyron, and Matthew were to take a small group of engineers, military dignities, and representatives from the Department of Defense, out of the bay for a short demonstration of the ship's capabilities.

Sam met Matthew's eye. The man was grinning as he gripped the small, wooden wheel, taking the *Tahila* out of the harbor.

"Well..." Sam said. "What do you think?"

"I can't say I haven't enjoyed my enforced vacation these past six months, but it's good to be back — and I think you've found a fair replacement for the *Maria Helena*."

Sam grinned. "I'm glad you approve. We went to some effort

to have her built."

"Sure," Matthew said, steering under the Coronado Bridge. "She's a beautiful ship, a technological marvel, but the Maria Helena had real class."

Sam expelled a breath. "Yeah, she sure, did."

The *Tahila* approached one of the wealthy marinas out from the Seaport Village. A large luxury motor cruiser by the name of *Carpe Diem* was in the process of motoring into the outside finger of the marina.

It was moving quicker than Sam would have expected given its size.

Sam raised his eyebrow. "What's the skipper trying to do?"

Matthew shook his head in disgust, shifting the throttles into reverse, to leave more room for the incoming vessel. "Beats me. Probably some rich kid playing with his family's yacht."

Sam's lips hardened. "Yeah, probably."

"No offense, Sam."

Sam shrugged. "None taken."

A moment later, the *Carpe Diem* struck the wall of the jetty hard.

The speed was low, and the ship appeared unscathed, although the owner would no doubt end up paying a fortune in repair bills to the marina.

Sam stared at the ship that now simply floundered next to the remains of the splintered jetty. His eyes narrowed.

Despite the destruction, nobody came out on deck.

Matthew said, "Where is everybody?"

Sam scanned the bridge. It looked barren.

He turned to Matthew. "You'd better take us a little closer."

CHAPTER TWENTY

MATTHEW BROUGHT THE BOW OF *Tahila* up to the aft deck of *Carpe Diem* and pulled the throttles back until both ships rested mere inches apart from one another.

Sam and Tom stepped across the gap and onboard *Carpe Diem*. Only the sound of the ship's diesel powerplant idling could be heard.

"Hello," Sam shouted. "Is anyone aboard?"

No response.

"Hello?" Sam repeated. "Is everyone all right?"

He and Tom exchanged glances.

Tom said, "I'll take the forward section."

"All right," Sam gripped the external ladder to the upper deck that housed the bridge. "I'll try the bridge."

He gripped the metal rungs of the ladder and climbed into the narrow space between the bridge and the steel balustrade.

Sam rapped his knuckles on the side of the glass door that led to the bridge. "Hey, is anyone in there?"

He cupped his hands over his eyes so that he could see

through the reflective glare of the forward windshield.

The sight turned his blood to ice.

He turned and raced down the ladder, shouting, "Tom! Stop!"

Tom met him at the lower deck. "What's up?"

The creases around Sam's face deepened. "They're all dead."

"Who's dead?"

"Everyone on board this boat," Sam said, his voice steady but hurried. "I don't know why. Their skin's all blistered. They look like they've been exposed to something toxic. Or maybe they're infectious."

Tom's cheerful voice hardened. "That means we might be infectious too."

"It's a possibility we've already been exposed to whatever it is." Sam looked up at the gentle ripples on the bay. The wind was picking up. "Look. If this boat is dangerous, we need to move it before that wind sweeps away all the toxins or whatever it was that killed those men."

Tom said, "All right. I'll get Genevieve to throw us down a couple FE suits. And then you and I will have to move her back off shore into quarantine until someone can work out what went wrong."

Sam nodded. "Sounds like a plan. Let's get this done quick."

CHAPTER TWENTY-ONE

SAM DONNED HIS YELLOW FE suit.

FE stood for Fully Encapsulated hazardous material suit. It was rated Level A, which was the highest level of protection against chemical, nuclear, and biological hazards by restricting any penetration by vapors, gases, mists, and particles. Sam switched on his tank of air and started to breathe from his Self-Contained Breathing Apparatus.

He turned to face Tom and gave him the thumbs up signal. "You okay?"

"Never better, you?"

"I'm all right. I'll be happier once I know what the hell's going on."

"Agreed."

Sam climbed the ladder up to the bridge. This time he was followed by Tom. He stopped at the door to the bridge, and checked the handle. It moved freely.

He glanced at Tom, who signaled with a curt nod that he was good to enter.

Sam turned the handle and opened the door.

Inside were two corpses—both men and starting to decompose.

There was no point checking either of them for signs of life. Instead, he consciously put them out of his mind, and made his way to the helm, where all maneuvering controls for the luxury motor yacht could be accessed.

It was the sort of helm that looked like it belonged to anything but a boat. Traditionalist sailors would have called it an affront. Sam couldn't care less what it looked like; he just wanted to work out how to get the *Carpe Diem* out to sea. Instead of a wheel, the ship had a single joystick—the same sort of thing a kid might use to play a video game—and instead of a simple pair of throttles for its twin engines, it used a touchscreen computer, with two digital towers representing the number of RPMs to give to each propeller.

At the center of the touchscreen were the words, *Forward, Neutral,* and *Back.*

To the right of that was an ECDIS screen, which stood for Electronic Chart Display and Information System. This provided geographic information for nautical navigation. It was synchronized with the ship's fully autonomous autopilot.

Sam tried to shift the digital gears into forward, but nothing happened. In fact, not only did the ship not move, but the computer gave him an immediate warning sound, as though he'd done something wrong.

He tried again with the same response.

"What the hell's wrong with this?" Sam asked.

Tom stood next him, his eyes sweeping the array of digital equipment. He pressed a button on the touchscreen which read, *New Waypoint.*

A cute little digital image of a ship appeared.

Sam watched as Tom placed his heavily gloved, impervious fingers on the touchscreen and dragged the ship's marker to a point two miles west of San Diego Bay.

He pressed enter.

Sam looked at him. "You're going to let the autopilot take this ship out to sea?"

The *Carpe Diem's* engines started roaring loudly as they increased RPM. The motor yacht slowly separated from the splintered jetty, making its way through the shipping channel of the harbor, and out to sea.

Tom met his eye. A small grin could only just be seen beneath his FE visor. "Hey, at least it's moving!"

Sam studied the rest of the bridge while the ship was under way, and Tom ducked down below to search for other survivors. The ship looked state of the art and immaculate. There was no sign of a fire, or drugs, or even alcohol. One person might have had a heart attack, but two? That seemed unlikely.

What the hell went wrong?

It was a short trip out to sea, lasting less than fifteen minutes, before the ship's engines eased into an idle and the computer applied a short burst of reverse thrust, bringing the ship to a complete standstill.

Sam pressed a button on the touchscreen and the electric motor whirred as the anchor and two hundred feet of chain rolled out of their cradle.

Tom came back up the internal stairs and opened the door. "There's no one else on board. Now what?"

"Now we wait for someone from the Navy's CBR emergency response team to come on board and tell us what the hell went wrong here."

Tom crossed his arms. "All right. Bet you I can find out the cause before they get here."

"How?"

"I don't know. Maybe there will be something obvious. Like a suicide note?"

Sam said, "The man owned a yacht probably worth a hundred million. I doubt he was the type."

"How would we know whether he was the type or not?"

Sam shrugged inside his FE suit. He was happy to play investigator while they wait. It might be hours before someone decides that they're safe to come off the boat. Until then, they were going to be stuck there.

He walked around the bridge, trying to see if there was anything that might provide some sort of explanation for the two deaths.

It was a long shot, and he found nothing unusual.

He squatted down and forced himself to look at the two bodies, thankful that he was wearing an FE suit with breathing apparatus, so he didn't have to smell the rotting remains. He let his mind take a morbid wonder. At a guess, he figured they must have been dead for a week or maybe even more. Either that or they had come from somewhere warm and humid, leading to a more rapid process of decomposition.

Sam brought up the navigational history log.

The previous trip had originated at Horse Shoe Island, within the Mergui Archipelago of the Andaman Sea, off the west coast of Thailand.

It made a single stop on the way, lasting a little under an hour, at a point a hundred and ten miles south of Guam, before cruising on autopilot all the way back to its home port in San Diego Bay.

Sam stared at the location on the map.

Why stop in the middle of nowhere out in the open ocean?

He felt Tom's hand on his shoulder. It was hard to hear people inside the FE suit over the sound of your breathing apparatus echoing inside the impervious material of the garment.

Sam asked, "What is it?"

Tom's face had turned hard. "I think I know why these two men are dead."

Sam's eyes narrowed. "You do?"

"Yeah they were poisoned."

"By what?"

"Carbon monoxide."

"Really?" Sam felt almost let down by the simple explanation. "How?"

"I noticed the air conditioning was blowing hot air. And I mean, really hot air. Enough so that I could feel it while inside my FE suit."

Sam shrugged. "Okay. So what? You really hate the heat. I get it."

"So, I adjusted the thermostat, and still the air conditioner blew hot air. You want to know why?"

Sam suppressed a smile. "Sure. I'll bite. Why?"

"I removed the grille, and you'll never believe what I found there..."

Sam said, "Go on!"

"Someone had hooked up the diesel engine's exhaust manifold — which appears to have been designed to be funneled through the ceiling and out the roof — to the air conditioning intake vent."

"Are you saying, whoever these two men are, they died because of a tragic maintenance accident?"

Tom nodded. "It would appear so."

Sam glanced down at the rotting bodies. "What a terrible waste of life."

He stepped over to the helm and switched off the engine.

After the drone of the twin diesel engines ceased, the *Carpe Diem* turned silent, like the ghost ship she'd become.

And then the tapping started.

CHAPTER TWENTY-TWO

SAM COCKED HIS EAR, TRYING to listen to the sound.
Inside the FE suit, it was near impossible to determine the location of something based on sound alone, because noise echoed inside.

He said, "Tom, can you hear that?"

Tom turned to look around the bridge, trying to guess what Sam was talking about. "Hear what?" he asked.

The tapping continued.

"That!" Sam said. "The tapping sound."

Tom paused. "Hey, I hear it too."

"What is that sound?"

"I don't know. Probably water from the impeller draining back out its piping now that the engines have been switched off, and there's no longer any driving force sucking the seawater in."

Sam stopped, listened to the sound some more.

It went three short tap, tap, taps... followed by three long tap, tap, taps...

He shook his head. "No. It's too regular. There's no way that's coming from the backflow of an impeller or any other water pipe."

Tom said, "Then what do you think it is?"

"I have no idea," Sam replied. "But I'm going to find out. It's coming from down below."

Sam stepped through the open door leading down the stairwell from the bridge into the main living and entertaining compartment of the large motor yacht. He followed the sound as best he could, toward the forward cabins.

The sound stopped.

He waited.

Nothing happened.

Sam waited and listened, becoming acutely aware of the sound of the breathing apparatus echoing inside his FE suit.

Then he heard it again.

Three short taps, followed by three long taps, followed again by three short taps.

"Holy shit!" He swore. "That's an SOS!"

He and Tom moved forward, opening the cabin door.

The cabin housed a king-sized double bed, lavatory, and a TV, but no people.

Again, the sound stopped.

Sam said, "Hello. Is anyone here?"

No answer.

"We're here to help. There's medical help on the way, too."

Silence.

"My name's Sam Reilly and my friend here is Tom Bower."

The silence was finally broken by the sound of more tapping.

It continued identically to the previous taps, producing the sound of SOS in Morse Code. Sam would have been hard pressed to remember much about Morse Code from his early induction days as a marine, but SOS was kind of a hard one to forget.

This sounded almost mechanical.

That was a more likely explanation than someone still being alive onboard.

The SOS tapping was interrupted by a thirty second pause, before starting again.

Sam looked at Tom and asked, "Where is that sound coming from?"

"I have no idea."

On the next round of taps, Sam turned to the locker next to the bed. The sound was definitely coming from inside.

"Hello," he said. "I'm Sam Reilly. I'm here to help."

The tapping stopped — two taps short of completing the SOS.

Sam reached for the door handle. It was locked from the outside. He slid the lock open.

He said, "I'm going to open the door now…"

Sam opened the heavy mahogany door.

A woman burst out immediately. She screamed as soon as she saw Sam and Tom in their yellow, alien-like, FE suits. Sam tried to hold her, but that just made her more hysterical and she started to lash out at him with her arms.

Sam removed the mask from his FE suit.

"It's all right," Sam said, holding her in his arms. "You're okay now. I promise."

She kept screaming.

"My name's Sam Reilly. Medical help is on its way. You're safe now."

The woman suddenly stopped fighting him. She didn't say anything. Sam glanced at her. She was tall, her blue eyes level with his own. She had multiple blisters all over her body, her dark brown hair was unkempt and disheveled, but there was a beauty in her face that was striking. More than that, he saw something else in her face, too.

What was it?

Hatred?

Determination?

Defiance?

Sam said, "You're safe now. Can you tell me what happened?"

The woman locked eyes with him and spoke. Her voice was sharp and unyielding. "Nothing's all right. They're going to kill us all."

Sam set his jaw. "Who are?"

Her voice was soft, more like a whisper. "The ones who came from the island!"

"What island?" Sam asked.

But the woman didn't answer.

Instead she started to fit. Her eyes rolled into the back of her head and her arms and legs stiffened. Her entire body shook in a tonic seizure.

Sam held her until her body stopped shaking.

He checked her carotid pulse. It was there, but it seemed weak to him, her breathing labored and irregular.

Sam looked at Tom. "Get on to that radio and let them know we have a casualty—but she's unconscious."

CHAPTER TWENTY-THREE

Scripps Mercy Hospital, San Diego

Sam Reilly sat on a single chair in the isolation room of the hospital with his fingers steepled in boredom. It wasn't that he didn't have things to do. He'd taken ownership of the *Tahila* less than eight hours ago, but already, there was a lot of work to be done—and none of it while he was trapped in isolation, waiting to discover what, if anything, his body had been exposed to. Everything he had in his possession when he boarded the *Carpe Diem*, including his clothes, and even his cell phone, had been taken away for decontamination.

That left him with nothing to use to search for answers. Instead, all he could do was replay in his mind the events of the past eight hours, in search of what had happened, what could now be done to deal with it, and what had to be done in terms of priorities providing the greatest good for the greatest amount of people.

What happened to the crew and owner of the *Carpe Diem* might all be attributed to careless maintenance and a tragic accident. If that ended up being the case, it would be the least harmful outcome. But what if it turned out to be something much more sinister? What if the ship harbored patient zero, and the first casualties in a potentially devastating pandemic?

He closed his eyes and thought about what type of circumstances could have led to the deaths of the two men on the bridge but kept the woman alive. More importantly, why had she survived, only to lapse into a seemingly permanent state of coma after he had freed her?

He pictured the scene he came across when he'd discovered her. The door had been locked from the outside. It was made of solid mahogany, meaning that it would have been nearly impossible to break through without any tools. The opposite side of the door led to a secret compartment, more than twenty feet wide, most likely designed for the storage of valuables. It reminded him of the wardrobe in C.S. Lewis's, *The Lion, the Witch, and the Wardrobe*. Inside, Tom told him there were significant food stores, so whatever happened to cause the woman to slip into a coma, it wasn't starvation or dehydration.

So, if that hadn't been the cause, the question remained, what was?

The sound of the negative pressure ventilation system, designed to draw air into the room thereby stopping any biological hazards from escaping, droned on in the background.

He opened his mind, his eyes staring blankly at the pale white wall. Why were hospital walls always so bland? Whose idea was it to make an isolation room entirely white? Did it add to the atmosphere of isolation?

Sam blinked, dismissing his rambling thoughts. None of it meant anything, certainly nothing he could do anything about while inside his self-inflicted medical prison. It was his own fault for removing his damned FE suit's mask.

He sighed heavily and grinned as he recalled the woman's

last words–

Beware the floating island of pumice…

That certainly got his attention. She might have been delirious, possibly even suffering the effects of low-level carbon monoxide poisoning, but a floating island of pumice isn't the sort of thing a disoriented and hypoxic brain tends to imagine.

No, there was some level of truth to that.

Sam's mind wandered toward the island of pumice. How tall could it be? How well did it float? He imagined an entire island of the light, porous volcanic rock. Pumice itself floated, but how about an entire island of the stuff? Would it drift like a gigantic iceberg? He considered the geology of the stone. It was created when super-heated, highly pressurized rock is violently ejected from a volcano. The gas-rich froth of glassy lava solidifies in an instant. The unusual foamy configuration of pumice occurs because of the simultaneous rapid cooling and depressurization.

But what did this tell him about the strange island?

His lips curled upward into a large grin. It told him that wherever this island was now, it originated at the sight of a volcanic eruption. More important yet, such an eruption must have been recent, because the light stone wouldn't remain conglomerated in an island forever. The constant wind, shifting waves, and conflicting currents would quickly cause it to disintegrate.

That meant that even if they knew where the *Carpe Diem* discovered the floating island of pumice, which they didn't, it would be near impossible to retrospectively calculate its current position. It would be like trying to find a needle in a haystack, after never really knowing where the haystack was in the first place.

But he could contact WOVO – the World Organization of Volcano Observatories – which might be able to provide a list of recent volcanic eruptions. In doing so, they might at least be able to narrow down their window a little better than somewhere within the Pacific Ocean.

He made a mental note to get Elise, his best researcher and computer expert, to contact WOVO and request a list of known volcanic eruptions in the past six weeks. And, failing that, any that might have had the potential to erupt without anyone noticing—such as on small unoccupied islands or atolls.

Sam stopped making a mental list of his tasks, because another doctor approached the entrance to his isolation room. Unlike the rest of the medical visitors he'd had, this one was wearing a white coat, and didn't stop to don a yellow biological hazard FE suit.

He grinned. It was a good sign.

He stood up to greet her. "Hello, Doc."

She smiled politely. It showed emotion, a genuinely kind smile, full of teeth. "Hello, Mr. Reilly, my name is Doctor Alyssa Smyth. I'm the medical director for infectious diseases at the CDC, but my background is in Chemical, Biological, and Radiation incidents, which is why I'm here, of course."

He took her in at a glance.

She looked far too young to be the medical director for the CDC, but he didn't say so. She had a beautiful face, not quite in the classical sense. Her hair was cut short, and tied back, more of an afterthought than an attempt to achieve any particular look. Her brown eyes were large, and her smile beguiling. She wore no makeup over her pale white skin. Her stature was decidedly short, emphasizing a full figure that was definitely heavier than the fashion magazines tell us we should like. Somehow for all her ordinariness, there was something striking about her.

"Pleased to meet you, Doctor Smyth," he said, shaking her hand. "Do you mind telling me which of those types of incidents this one falls under?"

Her face hardened. "Nuclear radiation, I'm afraid."

"The *Carpe Diem* was exposed to high levels of uranium radiation?"

She sat down next to him, leveled her eyes with his, and said, "No. Plutonium, actually."

"Good God." Sam swallowed hard. "How much was my exposure?"

"Small. About the same as forty standard days' worth of UV radiation. You'll live."

Sam expelled a breath. "What about the woman we found alive on the yacht?"

"Her name's Alicia Yeager, she was a guest of the owner of the vessel, a Mr. Travis Macintyre. She is suffering from acute radiation sickness. She's been exposed to roughly six Grays — which is a standardized measure of ionizing radiation exposure."

Sam asked, "Will she live?"

"It's hard to say. The dose she's been exposed to isn't particularly high. But it looks like it's been somewhere between a week to two weeks since she was first exposed, which means many of the symptoms are now manifesting, culminating in her cognitive decline, delirium and coma yesterday. We'll treat her with a drug called Prussian Blue, which binds to particles of the radioactive elements: plutonium, americium and curium. The radioactive particles then pass out of the body in urine, thereby reducing the amount of radiation absorbed."

"If I give you my cell number, can you please contact me as soon as she's awake? I need to talk to her, and find out what she knows."

"Of course, although I'm not making any promises she will ever wake up."

"I understand," Sam said. "Hey, why did it take so long for Alicia to deteriorate, when the two men on the bridge looked like they had died more than a week ago?"

Dr. Smyth referred to the report in her folder. "According to the forensic pathologist who conducted the autopsies, despite the fact they were exposed to the same amount of nuclear radiation as Ms. Yeager, both men died from carbon monoxide poisoning."

"Interesting. Why would someone try and poison them after they were exposed to high levels of radiation?"

"Why indeed?" she replied. "The most obvious guess to me is that they must have seen something they weren't supposed to see."

"Yeah. The question is what?" Returning to the bigger problem, Sam asked, "Are there any reports of a Broken Arrow—a misplaced or lost nuclear weapon?"

"No. I've made my report to the Pentagon directly. They're denying any possibility the plutonium has come from any nuclear weapons of ours, or anybody else's for that matter."

Sam cocked his eyebrow. "And you believe them?"

"Yeah, I do."

She spoke with the simple, confident, certainty of an expert in any given field. Her tone didn't change, as though she was trying to prove a point or debate the issue. It was merely stating a fact. She wasn't a politician hiding the truth, or lobbyist trying to promote their version of the truth, she was simply a leading expert in chemical, biological, and radiation disasters, expressing her opinion on what she had seen.

He suppressed a smile. "Why?"

"Because, we can already tell that this type of plutonium didn't come from a nuclear weapon."

"How do you do that?" It was a question, not a challenge.

"Weapons grade plutonium is highly refined. What we found on board the *Carpe Diem* was poor quality plutonium, mixed in with a number of fission byproducts, and transuranic elements—meaning it was the waste byproduct of nuclear energy production."

"Someone's been dumping nuclear waste somewhere they shouldn't be?"

"It looks like it."

"Any idea where?"

"No. In fact, we doubt the nuclear reactor is even still in service."

"Why?"

Dr. Smyth said, "Do you know much about nuclear power production?"

"Not a lot. The debate about its benefit for the planet has been hotly contested since the sixties, with those for it arguing that nuclear power is more efficient than coal, and therefore a cleaner source of energy."

She nodded. "A kilogram of uranium-235 converted via nuclear processes releases approximately three million times more energy than a kilogram of coal burned conventionally."

Sam shrugged. "Sure. But a kilogram of coal never accidentally turned into a nuclear meltdown, potentially killing millions, and leaving vast areas of the Earth uninhabitable for thousands of years."

"It does happen, but it's very rare these days. The fact remains, less people die from accidents involving nuclear power globally, than worldwide deaths that can be attributed to the effects of global warming, and poor breathable air quality as a result of coal power production. Besides, the inbuilt safety redundancy systems on modern nuclear power plants rarely fail."

"Try telling that to the families of those who lived and worked in the Fukushima Daiichi power plant?"

"I did."

"You did what?"

"I told the families of the workers at the Fukushima Daiichi Power Plant that it was extremely rare for a modern nuclear power plant to have this sort of disaster, only proving the need for humanity to move away from traditional energy sources of fuel and uranium, turning to greener sources."

Sam paused. His lips twisted in a wry grin of incredulity. "So you agree with me?"

"Mr. Reilly, I was part of the international nuclear advisory team that assisted during the Fukushima Daiichi Power Plant disaster. You don't need to convince me of the potential risks of nuclear power."

"Then why did you disagree with me about nuclear power?"

"I never disagreed with you. I simply wanted to make sure I had expressed all the facts before giving you my scientific conclusion."

He smiled. She was smart and funny... he liked that.

"So how can you tell what the plutonium came from?"

She sighed, unsure about how much she could be bothered explaining. Then, as though deciding to give Sam the benefit of the doubt, she said, "It has to do with the type of nuclear reactor."

"Go on, how?"

"Modern nuclear reactors designed for energy production are generally what are called thermal reactors, meaning they use a nuclear reactor to initiate and control a self-sustained nuclear chain reaction."

Sam said, "I'm still with you. Go on..."

"Most reactor designs in existence are thermal reactors and typically use water as a neutron moderator, which means that it slows down the neutrons to a thermal or slower speed, and they use the water as a coolant, of course. But in a fast breeder reactor, some other kind of coolant is used which will not moderate or slow the neutrons down much. This enables fast neutrons to dominate, which can effectively be used to constantly replenish the fuel supply. By merely placing cheap unenriched uranium into such a core, the non-fissionable U-238 will be turned into Pu-239." She met his eye, paused, and said, "Now, those on board the *Carpe Diem* were exposed to high levels of Pu-239."

Sam's eyes narrowed. "What are you saying?"

Her lips thinned into a hardline. "Modern nuclear reactors

use every last bit of plutonium produced as a means of maintaining the chain reaction."

"But?"

"Early nuclear reactors were never designed to efficiently produce energy. They were built to produce plutonium for weapons, using heavy water to collect the highly unstable radioactive isotopes." She looked at him, her eyes narrowing, as she tried to gauge how much he was following. "Early attempts to create nuclear reactions for electricity generation used heavy water, and thus wasted huge amounts of the highly unstable Pu-239 as a byproduct."

Sam said, "Are you telling me the *Carpe Deum* has recently somehow sailed past a pile of nuclear waste dumped from the sixties?"

"Yes, but I have no way of telling from our assessment of the vessel where that happened." She folded her arms across her chest. "I've spoken to the Secretary of Defense. She tells me that as soon as you're well enough to leave, it will be your job to find out. Although where you begin such a search, beats the hell out of me."

"Yeah, that makes two of us." Sam shook her hand again. "Thanks again, Doctor Smyth."

"You're welcome." Dr. Smyth handed him a bag. "Your clothes and cell phone have all been decontaminated. I've left you my contact details, in case you need any further assistance. Let me know what you find out. I'm keen to learn."

"For sure, you'll be the first one I call."

She glanced at him, holding her gaze a moment longer than was natural. "Good luck, Mr. Reilly."

"Thank you, Dr. Smyth."

"I'm not your doctor anymore. You can call me Alyssa."

Sam smiled. "Thank you, Alyssa."

Sam watched her go, wondering what the rules were on doctors dating people who were no longer their patients. It was a fleeting thought. A curiosity. Nothing more. But there was something alluring about Alyssa that intrigued him.

He picked up his cell phone.

There was a message from Elise — ALICIA YEAGER POSTED THIS ON SOCIAL MEDIA TEN DAYS AGO.

He clicked open to download the high-resolution image.

Inside was a picture of a large, floating island of pumice.

CHAPTER TWENTY-FOUR

THE *TAHILA* RACED WEST OUT into the Pacific Ocean at full speed.

Sam stood at the helm, holding onto the wheel, enjoying the sheer pleasure of the ship's raw power, speed, and agility, as she gracefully danced over the surface. He would have liked to go up onto the deck, but given their speed, that was entirely out of the question. Shaped like a bullet, the *Tahila* skimmed and pierced the waves.

Matthew, Sam's skipper, stood next to him, his eyes rapt with pleasure at the way the new ship handled.

Sam asked, "What do you think?"

"I think she's an abomination to traditional sailing, but if you're going to embrace all this technology, then you've got to do it all the way. She's more like a rocket ship than a cruiser."

"Yeah, she's a delight to handle," Sam acknowledged. "Somehow it's what I imagine it would be like to drive a racecar—there's more power than you could ever know what to do with."

He handed the helm back to Matthew, who refused to put it

onto autopilot yet. Instead, he took the wheel, and enjoyed the experience. Sam laughed, wondering how far along their journey into the Pacific Ocean it would take before he lost interest and switched back to fully autonomous control.

"Good bye, Matthew. I'm going to go talk to Veyron."

"Good luck, Sam. Veyron's like a kid in a candy store, admiring and working his way through the various assessments of each of his new diving machines."

"Good. Because that's exactly what I need to talk to him about."

Sam headed aft, along the internal passageways, before taking a set of internal stairs down into the dive locker. Here Veyron was working his way through a series of tests for the new Triton 36,000/3 three-person submarine. It was an updated version of the old Sea Witch II that was destroyed when the *Maria Helena* was torpedoed.

Veyron climbed out of the little submarine's cockpit. "Hey Sam. Anything I can do for you?"

"There might be," Sam said. "What do you think of the new ship?"

"She's great. My office down here's a lot nicer in many ways. In particular, I don't end up getting soaked every so often by the moonpool like I used to. But all said and done, I'll miss the old girl. She was a solid and reliable ship."

"Yeah, she sure was," Sam said with a sigh.

Veyron climbed off the submarine and gave Sam's hand a firm shake. "Now, you didn't come down here just to reminisce about the *Maria Helena*, did you?"

"No."

"All right, what is it then?"

"As you know, we've been tasked to locate where this mysterious island of pumice—covered in nuclear radioactive waste—originated."

Veyron said, "I believe a volcano is traditionally where pumice originates."

"Exactly, which is what I wanted to talk to you about. We're heading toward the Mariana Trench."

Veyron nodded, slowly following what he was getting at. "You think a rogue nuclear nation has been dumping its nuclear waste into the depths of the Mariana Trench?"

"That's the working hypothesis we're running on," Sam admitted. "We've been tasked to locate the source of the high concentration of nuclear radiation. If it was, as you suggested, dumped in the Mariana Trench, it might have been all right for thousands of years — unless…"

Veyron sighed heavily. "A submerged volcano erupted, sending hundreds of tons of nuclear waste to the surface in the form of volcanic froth — AKA an island of floating, nuclear, pumice."

"Now you're getting it."

"Which means, you want me to make sure the Triton submersible is ready for a deep dive?"

"Afraid so," Sam said.

Veyron asked, "All right, when do we arrive?"

"Another forty-eight hours."

"I guess you want it to carry three persons on board?"

Sam said, "You guess right."

"Okay, it will be ready."

Sam stood up. "Thanks Veyron."

"Hey Sam?"

"Yeah?"

"Will Tom and Genevieve be returning in time for the dive?"

"No. At this stage they're heading to Horse Shoe Island, within the Mergui Archipelago off the coast of Myanmar."

"Why?"

"That was the last landfall the *Carpe Diem* stopped at before cruising on autopilot all the way back to its home port in San Diego Bay — with the exception of a single stop for an hour somewhere in the open waters above the Mariana Trench."

Veyron thought about that for a moment. "All right. Stay safe. You know we normally count on Tom to stop you doing something stupid."

"I know. I'll try my best."

Sam climbed the series of internal stairs, and headed forward to the command center.

Elise met him in the passageway. "Hey Sam, Aliana Wolfgang's on the satellite phone. She says she needs to speak to you about the results… something about a blood-stained shirt?"

Sam nodded. "Thank you. I've been waiting for them."

"Where do you want to take the call?"

"Send it through to my quarters. I'll head there now."

"Okay."

Sam made his way to his quarters. The ship used an internal phone system, which could be used to communicate to any section of the ship, as well as being connected to the satellite dish on the top deck.

Aliana Wolfgang was one of the leading microbiologists in the world, a director and highest shareholder of Wolfgang Incorporated and Pharmaceutical Research Lab—and she just happened to share an on-again off-again type relationship with Sam.

There was a time he would have gladly married her. Still would, but she wouldn't have him. She had said that she would constantly be worried that he wouldn't come home one day. That the world needed heroes, it really did, but heroes didn't get to grow old, and that wasn't how she wanted to live her life. In the end, they had remained close friends, separated by vastly different lives. But every now and again those lives would intersect and they would spend a few wonderful days together.

The red light of an incoming call flashed intermittently.

He picked it up. "Hello, Aliana."

CHAPTER TWENTY-FIVE

S AM WAITED.

There was a slight delay on the satellite line.

"Sam!" Aliana said, her tone soft. "Where are you?"

"The Pacific Ocean... um... about four hundred miles east of Micronesia."

"Why?"

"I'm heading to the waters off the coast of Guam, trying to locate where a rogue nuclear nation has been dumping nuclear waste."

There was a pause, then Aliana's cheerful voice. "Of course you are. That makes sense."

Sam asked, "Aliana, did you get my blood-stained shirt?"

"I got it Sam. I did what you asked and had a sample of the blood analyzed and the results compared with the known DNA records of Amelia Earhart to see if they are indeed related."

Sam found himself involuntarily holding his breath. "What did you find?"

"You're not going to believe this."

"The match is close?"

Aliana said, "No. Not close. Exactly the same."

Sam stared out the translucent wall, watching the waves roll by.

He waited for a moment, as his mind silently processed the new information. "Can you have identical DNA between mother and daughter, or a skipped generation… say someone and their grandmother?"

"No. Not identical. Your DNA is shared between your parents."

His lips twisted into a wry grin. "What are you saying, Aliana?"

"I don't know where you got that blood from, but it wasn't a descendant of Amelia Earhart, that's for certain."

He bit his lower lip. "Then what was it?"

"It was Amelia Earhart's blood."

With his heart in his throat, Sam asked, "How can that be?"

Aliana said, "I analyzed something else. She has the same type of progressively lengthening telomeres found in the chromosomes of Ben Gellie's blood sample." Sam recalled his dreadful kidnapping experience with Ben Gellie recently.

"Are you telling me she's a descendant of the Master Builders?"

"No. These are decidedly different from Ben Gellie's. There have been synthetic changes. More like her DNA sequence has been synthetically altered."

"How?"

Aliana said, "I have no idea."

CHAPTER TWENTY-SIX

―――――=ll∞⟨⟩⟨⟩⟨⟩∘ll=―――――

Horse Shoe Island, Myanmar

THE CESSNA 162 SKYCATCHER FLEW high above the Andaman Sea.

The light sports aircraft was never designed to be used as a seaplane, but someone in Myanmar had swapped its wheels for a pair of floats, and the aircraft was now being used as a private transporter to shuttle tourists to the remote atoll known as Horse Shoe Island. It was the low tourist season, and Tom had managed to negotiate hiring the aircraft for a few days.

Horse Shoe Island came into view up ahead. Large limestone mountains curved around to form its name's shape, enclosing a dense jungle and a white sandy beach at the center, overlooking azure and turquoise waters. The place was home to the Moken people—a tribe of ancient seafarers—who had used the island to fish and collect materials to build their kabangs for hundreds of years. It was said that the Moken people, who lived most of their lives out at sea, shared an intrinsic relationship with the ocean. If anyone knew about a strange island of pumice in the

Mergui Archipelago, it would be the Moken people.

Tom banked to the left, setting up to do a reconnaissance flypast to rule out any floating logs, small boats, sand bars, or surface debris inside the calm turquoise waters of the main lagoon. He dropped his height, flying through the entrance to the mountains, staying just above the water, before pulling back on the wheel and climbing out of the lagoon over the limestone mountains.

Next to him, Genevieve, turned and said, "Okay, now this is more like it. For once, Sam has really sent us on a vacation."

"It was kind of him. He did mention he'd like us to locate a deadly island of floating radioactive pumice while we're here though."

Genevieve stretched back in her seat, folding her arms over her lap. She looked like the epitome of the vacationing tourist, relaxed and comfortable. She had brown hair which she wore short, giving her an almost elf-like appearance. She wore a blue singlet that accentuated her lithe, muscular arms, and slim figure and a pair of short cargo pants. Despite her appearance, she was one of the deadliest women – or men – on Earth.

Her dark blue eyes scanned the beach with interest, and she smiled. "Suit yourself. We'll find the island of nuclear pumice, message Sam, and get back to our vacation."

Tom banked again, bringing the Skycatcher around for its final approach. "No reason we can't enjoy ourselves, too, darling."

"Good. Just so we're in agreement about that."

Tom flew a sharp, 180 degree turn, entering the main lagoon via the seaward access route. He set the flaps to thirty degrees, reduced power, and brought the Cessna Skycatcher into a glide. Using peripheral vision for cues, he observed the height of the trees on shore, his eyes carefully observing the ripples on the water.

Just above the surface, he raised the nose. This made the

aircraft flare, meaning to lose lift and stall, slowing its descent, causing its twin pontoons to softly hydroplane for a moment before they sank gently into the water.

Several long-tailed boats were anchored up against the sandy shore, with a couple Moken kabangs pulled up on the beach.

Tom taxied the seaplane toward the island's single jetty.

Genevieve climbed out and tied the floats up to a set of cleats on the jetty with a series of mooring lines, before giving Tom the thumbs up signal.

Tom reduced the engine to an idle, before powering off. The engine coughed and the propeller stopped spinning. He unclipped his harness, opened the door, and took in a deep breath of the warm, tropical air.

Genevieve stepped up to him, wrapped her arms around his neck, and kissed him on the lips. "Island of deadly floating pumice or not, this still looks like paradise to me."

CHAPTER TWENTY-SEVEN

Pacific Ocean, South of Guam

THE CONSTANT DRUM OF THE *Tahila's* powerful twin diesel engines came to a rest 12 miles south of Guam. Approximately 6.8 miles of water below her keel rested on the southernmost tip of the Mariana Trench. Despite being the deepest known location of any ocean in the world the water this morning was as flat as a millpond; the only small ripples seen were those caused by the wake of the ship.

Sam Reilly stepped out onto the upper deck, to set his eyes on it.

The weather was warm and deceitfully comforting. Matthew and Veyron followed him topside.

"There's nearly seven miles of seawater below our keel gentlemen," Sam said, his voice slow, almost reverent. "Compare that to the final resting place of the RMS Titanic, which was a cool 3.5 miles or a relative breeze by comparison with current submersible technologies, and you get some perspective about the area we've been asked to search."

Veyron's downturned eyes looked up to see more than a hundred flying fish leave the calm water and spiral into the air, while the giant tuna jumped out of the water to feed on them. "More people have walked on the moon than reached its depth."

"And only mankind would be dumb enough to even consider dumping nuclear waste in such a place," Sam said. "Yet, in 2015 that's exactly what was suggested at a United Nations meeting on sustainable storage of nuclear waste."

Matthew's jaw hardened. "That's insane."

"Yeah, it was. And, finding reason, the UN council vetoed the proposal as being reckless with the potentially catastrophic results being impossible to manage due to its severe depth. But if the *Carpe Diem* did in fact come across radioactive material in a floating nearby island of pumice, then it suggests someone didn't agree to the UN's veto."

Matthew asked, "Do we have any evidence of that fact, yet?"

Sam shook his head. "No. That's what we've been asked to gather."

"The Mariana Trench is a big place. How do you propose you're going to narrow the location down?"

"We'll be leaving a series of floating Geiger Counters, designed to pick up and measure any ionizing radiation in the form of alpha particles, beta particles, and gamma rays." Sam ran his eyes across the still water. "The *Tahila* will be running deep water bathymetry, searching for any large changes in the seabed—specifically looking for any recent evidence of the eruption of a submerged volcano."

"Have there been any reports of seismic activity?" Veyron asked.

"Yes. Two weeks ago, a measuring station set up on Guam recorded enormous amounts of energy in line with a large tectonic shift. Some bright minds at the Pentagon who have analyzed the data tell me that energy like that could only come from three known sources: an erupting volcano, a tectonic shift, or an atomic bomb."

"So this must be the right location?" Veyron said.

"Possibly…" Sam replied. "And possibly not. The Mariana Trench is located where the Pacific and Philippine tectonic plates converge, meaning powerful tectonic shifts are very common in the region. Our job is to find out if this is something different."

"Understood," Matthew and Veyron replied in unison.

"That's what I was thinking. Let's get to it then gentlemen."

CHAPTER TWENTY-EIGHT

THE *TAHILA* FOLLOWED A GRID, searching that stretched along a region ten miles north and south along the Mariana Trench from the known location where the *Carpe Diem* stopped mid-ocean for an hour for no apparent reason.

The Mariana Trench is a crescent-shaped trough in the Earth's crust, roughly 1,580 miles long, and 43 miles wide. The maximum known depth is 36,070 feet along the southern end of a slot shaped valley, known as Challenger Deep.

Inside the ship's command center, Sam watched the array of computer monitors, taking in the data from a collection of sources, including Geiger Counters, sea temperature gauges, and bathymetric readings of the shape of the seabed far below. Of the three of these, only the third one, the bathymetric readings were particularly interesting to watch on the screens. The Geiger Counters and thermometers would sound an alarm if they received data outside normal parameters.

Matthew stood at the helm, which was set on autopilot to follow the specific grid course, while he maintained watch.

Sam said, "Did you know, if Mount Everest was dropped into the trench at this point, its peak would be 1.2 miles under water?"

Matthew shook his head. "No. As a sailor, I've always aimed to remain on the surface of the ocean, giving very little thought to any additional room beneath the keel."

Sam wasn't easily dissuaded by his apathy on the topic. "Do you know what part of the seafloor is closest to the center of the Earth?"

Matthew rolled his eyes, clearly unimpressed by the concept. "Yeah, the seafloor beneath the Arctic, because the Earth is not a perfect sphere, its radius is about 16 miles smaller at the poles than at the equator."

Sam grinned. "Hey, you were paying attention in school…"

"Sure I did, I'm just not interested in quizzes in an age when we have Google!"

Sam continued watching the bathymetric readout along the computer monitor. The system used a multibeam echosounder — AKA a really good sonar — to measure the topography of the ocean floor surrounding the trench.

The Mariana Trench is part of the Izu-Bonin-Mariana subduction system that forms the boundary between two tectonic plates. As the Pacific and Philippine plates converge, they carry seamounts — mountains on the ocean floor that don't reach the water's surface — and other underwater features with them toward the trench itself. Some of these plow into other structures on the opposite side of the trench in a sort of slow-motion seamount collision, or into the trench wall itself.

In this process, an underwater bridge forms, stretching across the Mariana Trench. So far, there have been four such bridges documented, some as high as 7000 feet above the trench and measuring 47 miles long.

After nearly forty-eight hours of tracking the grid search, the *Tahila* started to run low on diesel. As arranged earlier, they headed to the US Navy base on Guam to refuel. Boredom set in, and Sam started to read a new book on the top deck. It was a new one by one of his favorite authors, James D. Grant. He was about a third of the way through it when he headed downstairs to check their progress.

He entered the command center and stopped.

The echosounder had been left running and the bathymetric display still drifted across the monitor. The entire region was riddled with seamounts and guyots — flat-topped seamounts — but in front of him was a section of the Mariana Trench seafloor that was almost completely flat.

Sam's eyes narrowed.

He pulled back the chair, and examined the image on the screen.

He turned to Matthew and shouted, "Full stop!"

Because in the middle of the near complete flatness, he spotted a large volcano — and next to that, a perfectly formed sphere.

CHAPTER TWENTY-NINE

The Sphere–Mariana Trench

SAM GRIPPED THE HOLD BAR next to the bathymetry station. The *Tahila*'s quad HamiltonJet waterjets rotated their direction 180 degrees, slowing the vessel as though someone had just jammed on the brakes.

The Geiger Meter alarm went off, followed by the thermal alert. The area surrounding the sphere was filled with nuclear radiation which was releasing heat. Sam felt his heart pound in his chest. Someone had really done it. They had dumped nuclear waste at the bottom of the Mariana Trench. It might be years old, its toxic materials only being released to the surface after a recent eruption of a nearby submerged volcano.

When the *Tahila* came to a complete standstill in the water, Matthew stood next to Sam and stared at the bathymetric read out. Sam increased the frequency of the sonar bursts, upping the resolution of the image.

Matthew said, "Holy shit! What is that?"

"Beats the hell out of me. The thing looks like a sphere,

partially buried in the seabed." Sam's lips twisted into a grin. "I don't suppose you know what causes a natural sphere to form at the bottom of the sea?"

Matthew shook his head. "Strange underwater phenomena are meant to be your area of expertise."

Sam stared at the monitor.

A sphere.

What the hell forms a perfect sphere in nature?

One of the most beautiful mathematical formations found in nature is the perfect sphere. A perfect sphere is defined as being completely symmetrical around its center, with all points on the surface lying the same distance from the center point. While Earth is often referred to as a sphere, it actually just misses this classification because it is slightly squashed at the poles. Nonetheless, perfect spheres do appear in nature and can be seen in examples such as bubbles, water drops, planets, and atoms. The sun itself is considered to be an almost perfect sphere.

But nothing should make a perfect sphere at the bottom of the ocean.

He took a screen capture of the strange spherical shape. The contours were derived by an array of sonar *sound pings,* meaning there was no way to physically see what it looked like.

But he could calculate how big it was by using a known height. He brought up the precise depth of the seafloor. 36,035 feet. Then, dragging the sonar icon to the very top of the sphere, he took a second reading. This one came back at 35, 035 feet, giving the sphere a diameter of 1000 feet and a radius of 500 feet.

Sam opened up the calculator app on the computer.

He applied the data to the formula — $V = \square/3\ \pi r^3$, and pressed enter.

He gasped as he saw the sphere's volume:

523,598,775.5983 cubic feet.

He picked up the satellite phone and dialed the Secretary of Defense direct.

She picked up on the second ring. "What have you found, Mr. Reilly?"

CHAPTER THIRTY

―――――⫯⫯∞⟨⟩⟨⟩∞⫯⫯―――――

SAM AND HIS CREW SPENT the next eight hours trying to gather as much information as possible from the sphere. But there was only so much they could gather from the surface. To find out what it really was, they were going to need to go down there.

Matthew stepped beside Sam. "Our guests will be arriving any minute now if you want to meet them up on the deck, or do you want me to go?"

Sam stood up. "No. I'll greet them. Thanks, Matthew."

He climbed the series of steps up onto the top deck, next to the helipad.

His satellite phone rang as soon as he was outside.

It was Tom Bower.

"Tom. How did it go? Did you find the island of pumice?"

"No. It's not here," Tom replied. "I spoke with a local guide who took me to a nearby Moken flotilla. The guide said that the Moken are so well aligned with the sea, that they know if there's a problem well before it starts."

"And?"

"They say they've never seen a floating island before."

"They're certain?"

"Yeah. If they had, it would be the sort of news that everyone would have heard about."

"That's good to know," Sam said. "It means we don't need to be worried about clearing out the region to avoid a major catastrophe."

"Any luck on your end?"

"We've found what we believe are the origins of the deadly pumice island. There's a large volcanic mound in the base of the Mariana Trench. Submerged Geiger Counters indicate radiation levels are through the roof."

"Wow. Someone really went through with it?"

"Dumping nuclear waste in the Mariana Trench?"

"Yeah."

"It would appear so."

Tom said, "We can organize a flight to Guam tonight, and help with the dive in forty-eight hours."

"That's all right, finish your vacation. I wouldn't want to cut Genevieve short on what's owed to the two of you."

"Are you sure?"

Sam said, "Yeah. The Pentagon is sending me a nuclear expert and some other witness who wants a firsthand visual. So the Trident submarine won't have room for a second pilot."

"You're sure?"

"Yeah. Go, have fun."

Sam hung up.

In the distance, he heard the whir of a Eurocopter UH-72 Lakota. Sam watched it approach. He took a step back, waiting for it to alight. The pilot landed with the speed and precision expected of Navy aviators. The rotor blades kept turning, while two people climbed out, and with ducked heads, came to meet him.

A moment later, the Navy chopper took off, returning to its base in Guam.

He turned to his distinguished guests.

One of the passengers was a man he'd never met before. The man greeted him with a firm handshake. "I'm Major James Marazzato, Military Intelligence. And this is…"

Sam smiled and turned to face the woman. "Hello, Dr. Alyssa Smyth. It's good to see you again."

CHAPTER THIRTY-ONE

Sam showed both guests the data.

Dr. Smyth said, "I don't get it. Are you trying to tell me the radiation isn't coming from the sphere?"

Sam nodded. "Yeah. At first we thought it was, but as we've been able to position submerged Geiger Meters closer to the sphere, it's become obvious that whatever nuclear material has been dumped down there, it's in this sunken area to the north of the sphere."

James said, "Do you have any idea what that sphere is?"

Sam crossed his arms. "I'm sorry. We don't have a clue."

Dr. Smyth asked, "Any chance it's natural?"

Sam thought about that for a moment. "Like a unique giant clam shell or something?"

"Yeah, why not?" the doctor replied.

"It's always a possibility, although highly unlikely. We know there is a unique array of extremophiles living at that depth that no one would have ever predicted, so it's not impossible to imagine that a creature like the sphere might have once lived. But there's one reason that makes me suspect it's man-made."

James asked, "And what's that?"

Sam said, "It's a perfect sphere."

"So?"

"You don't find a lot of perfect spheres in nature. Don't get me wrong, they do exist, however most of the time, they're very much spherical, but not perfect." Sam glanced up toward the sky. "The sun is a perfect sphere. Bubbles have the potential of forming into a perfect sphere. But for the most part, gravity and other competing factors cause a sphere to be slightly heavier on one side or the other."

James frowned, immediately seeing the implications. "But this one isn't?"

Sam sighed. "No. This one's perfect."

"Which means, this has been built by someone." James crossed his arms. "If someone else has the technology to build a sphere of this size at the bottom of the Mariana Trench, you know what that means?"

"Yep," said Sam. "We've already lost the technology race."

Alyssa said, "Why? There's nothing that suggests it's a weapon."

"No." Major Marazzato met her eye. "But it doesn't have to be. The fact is any species capable of building such a machine is so much farther advanced than us, it makes any weapons we have obsolete."

"Why?" Alyssa persisted.

Sam said, "It's like this. The pressure exerted on anything at the depth at the bottom of the trench is 1,086 bars, or more than a thousand times the standard atmospheric pressure at sea level. By comparison, the borosilicate dome of the submarine downstairs is one of three capable of reaching that depth without imploding—and it has a diameter of just 7.5 feet. Making something with a 1000-foot diameter, that could withstand the pressure, is practically impossible in terms of human capability."

The doctor's eyes narrowed. "What are you saying, Mr. Reilly?"

Major Marazzato set his jaw firm. "He's saying technology like that didn't come from Earth."

CHAPTER THIRTY-TWO

There was no doubt, given what was at stake, that they needed to reach the sphere now, before anyone else beat them to it. If it was indeed alien technology, they couldn't risk anyone else reaching it before them.

The Triton 36,000/3 submersible was fueled and ready to dive. In addition to the submarine's long list of capabilities, this one had been specifically modified to provide life-support for three occupants, for a total of five days.

Sam briefed his two guests on the plan for the dive, and the submarine's multiple redundancy systems.

Walking around the submarine he pointed to the locks that held the borosilicate dome to the submersible's main dual pontoons, which housed the submarine's battery modules, additional gas supplies, and computers.

Sam said, "In an emergency, we can manually decouple the central dome and the sub's pontoons, sending us on a fast, one way nonstop trip to the surface."

"What if the pressure jams the coupling?" Dr. Smyth asked.

"It's unlikely. The submarine's been designed to compensate

for that."

Her lips thinned. "Yes, but has it ever been tested at 36,000 feet?"

"No," Sam admitted. "It's been down to the Challenger Deep trench, but no one has ever tested the safety release system at that depth before. And we shouldn't have to, either."

She nodded, accepting, but unimpressed by his answer.

Sam walked around to the side of the submarine. Getting on his knees, he pointed out two large lead weights at the bottom of each pontoon.

He said, "This is attached to the hull via a sodium crystal anode. Basically, as soon as the anode touches the water, it starts to destabilize. After five days in the water, at the limit of our life-support capabilities, it loses all strength, releasing the weighted ballast, sending us straight back to the surface."

Dr. Smyth smiled. "A redundancy for the redundancy. I like that. It's one thing to get crushed in a split second, but quite another to remain trapped at the bottom of the ocean forever, to die a terrible suffocating death."

"This submarine is extremely capable, and Veyron maintains it to perfection," Sam said. "Besides, if you're going to worry about anything, I'd be concerned about the nuclear radiation, and where it's going."

"Or that damned sphere," Major Marazzato said. "Who built it, who owns it, and where the hell is it going?"

Sam finished off his safety checks and said, "All right, if everyone's ready, let's go."

Matthew stepped into the dive locker. The fine creases around his face were somehow deeper, and more defined. "You might have a problem."

"What is it?" Sam asked.

"I've just received a weather warning from Guam about the risk of an incoming cyclone."

Sam took a breath. "How certain are you it's going to reach

us?"

Matthew placed the synoptic, meteorological, and hydrological charts on the table next to Sam. "There's no doubt about if it's going to reach here; it's a matter of when."

Sam glanced at the reports. There was a category five cyclone heading their way. It was so large that Sam could not question Veyron's conclusion. "Have you contacted anyone about this?"

"Yeah, I've spoken to our meteorologist in New Zealand. He's confirmed it will hit our current location in three days."

"What does that mean for the dive?" Major Marazzato asked, his tone hard and determined, without suppressing his urgency to dive. "Can we still dive?"

Sam turned to Matthew. "It shouldn't be a problem. It's a seventy-five minute dive to the bottom, and two hours back up again. Even if we spend another twenty hours down there taking photos, video recordings, and samples, it still leaves another forty-eight hours to get back here. Within that time, the *Tahila* can have us hundreds of miles away."

"What if you encounter a problem while you're down there?" Matthew asked. "Would it be more prudent to wait until after the cyclone?"

"Worst case scenario, we'll stay at the bottom for five days until the storm passes, and then surface."

"You'll be on your own when you get topside. We'll be bunkered down hundreds of miles away, but we can come back for you as soon as the cyclone passes."

Sam nodded. "It's still a worst-case scenario. I think the risk is acceptable."

"We have other pressing reasons to reach that sphere before the storm," Major Marazzato said. "Like beating any other nation from finding it first. If we don't dive now, how long until we can make another one?"

Sam answered, "It might be a while. This is the first cyclone for the season. It usually sets off the cyclone season, meaning it might be three or four months before we get another good window to dive. I'm happy to take the risk."

Dr. Smyth sighed, and said, "All right, I vote we take the risk."

CHAPTER THIRTY-THREE

Diving to the Deepest Trench on Earth

SAM FELT THE SUBMARINE SHIFT as he strapped himself into the pilot seat. He quickly ran through the cross-check start up procedure using the mnemonic HACHIT—checking the Hatch, Air supply, Controls, Harnesses, Instruments and Trim.

Outside, Veyron confirmed that everything was set to dive.

Sam waited until Veyron climbed off the back of the submarine and then asked, "Are we ready to get this sub in the water?"

"You're good," Veyron confirmed.

"Thanks." Sam turned to his two passengers. "You happy, Dr. Smyth?"

She folded her hands across her lap. "Happy as I ever am when I approach the site of a nuclear disaster."

Sam turned to his left. "How about you, Major?"

"I'm just glad we're going to be the first to lay eyes on that sphere."

Sam flicked on the running lights. "All right. Systems all check out. We're good to go."

Sam depressed the radio transmitter. "*Tahila*, this is *Sea Witch II*, we're good for launch."

"Sorry, Sam," Matthew replied over the radio. "I didn't catch the new name for the Triton submersible."

Sam looked out the windshield, toward Veyron, his palms pointed skyward, he yelled, "What's her name?"

Veyron shrugged. "We haven't named her, yet."

Sam nodded. "Okay Tahila, sorry about the confusion. This is *Ursula*, we're ready for launch."

There was a pause on the radio.

Then Matthew replied, "Copy that *Ursula*, safe journey to the bottom. We'll see you in twenty-four hours. Good luck."

In front of them, Veyron adjusted the controls for the dive elevator. "All right, everyone, here you go."

Sam felt his gut shift uncomfortably in his seat as *Ursula* was lowered beneath the lockout hatch beneath the keel. Instead of being dropped into the water, she was now positioned inside her elevator-like cradle beneath the water and well below *Tahila's* hull. Still connected to the elevator, she looked like a sports car parked in a tight space.

Sam depressed the release button and then gently pushed the joystick forward. The array of electric motors whirred into life, and *Ursula* moved quickly out of her cradle. He dipped the joystick, gently dropping another thirty or so feet.

Above them, he stared at the lowered elevator, extending from *Tahila's* spacecraft-like hull and keel, like a wart. He pressed another button and the elevator retracted inside the ship's lockout hatch, leaving the hull trim once more.

Not forgetting his passengers, Sam said, "Welcome to the world under the sea."

Dr. Smyth said, "We're not rocking back and forth anymore."

"No." Sam flicked the ballast switch. Water began flooding into the tanks, while air bubbles gurgled to the surface. "If you want speed, you need to be on top of the water, but for comfort, the best place is always down below."

Dr. Smyth smiled. There was mischief in her eyes, and her rosebud like mouth teased him. "There are no waves to contend with?"

"Exactly."

Ursula took on water, and began to sink quickly.

It would take just seventy-five minutes to reach the seabed a little less than seven miles from the surface. The submarine descended fast, but there was little to show for their progression. By maintaining an internal pressure of one atmosphere throughout the entire dive, and with very little marine life or visual cues, there was no sense of altered depth.

At a thousand feet, Sam depressed the mike and said, "*Ursula* to *Tahila*, we've reached a thousand feet. Please confirm communication's cable is intact?"

"We're reading you five out of five, Sam," Matthew acknowledged. "Stay safe."

Major Marazzato tapped Sam on the shoulder. "I didn't realize you had communications this far down... something about water being a poor conductor of sound waves."

Sam grinned. "Actually, it's a great conductor. The real problem with underwater communication is that because of the increased conductivity, it will tend to disperse the wave and attenuate the signal that gets through."

The Major frowned. "So then, how are you communicating with the surface ship?"

"We're attached to a communications umbilical cord, tethered to *Tahila*. That way, people topside can keep us up to date if there are any drastic changes to the weather, we can keep an open coms line, and also they will be able to receive a direct video and audio feed from the submarine."

Major Marazzato's brow furrowed. Sam watched the man shift uncomfortably in his seat. "They're streaming a direct video feed of everything we can see?"

"Yeah," Sam said, his tone intentionally cheerful. "Is that going to be a problem?"

"No problem."

Sam scanned the array of digital gauges. They passed the 3,000 foot depth mark, entering the aphotic *midnight zone,* in which sunlight no longer penetrated, and the view from the borosilicate dome was now bathed in darkness.

He flicked another switch and two powerful LED lights came on, revealing very little in the way of marine life outside. Confident there was nothing to be seen until they neared the seabed miles below, Sam switched the lights off to conserve the energy they used.

Sam said, "Okay, if you want a rest, now's your time to take it. There won't be anything to see for the next hour. Next stop, the bottom of the Mariana Trench."

CHAPTER THIRTY-FOUR

Major James Marazzato sat back uncomfortably in his allotted seat toward the portside of the tiny submersible. At six foot three he was by far too tall to be at ease in the craft. He was just thankful that he had chosen a profession that seldom required him to descend in an elongated coffin.

For the first twenty minutes he attempted to see out.

The marine life was fairly sparse after they had passed the first five hundred feet, in which swarms of flying fish could be seen. Below that there was little to see. When they reached three thousand feet Sam turned on the outer lights, but the view didn't particularly improve.

When Marazzato looked out, all he could see was the constant movement of water over the submersible, then after a time it was hard to imagine that it was even moving at all.

"Okay gents, I'm switching external lights off to conserve energy." He heard Sam Reilly's automatic notes.

Marazzato tried to get some sleep. He would need to conserve his energy for the time spent on the bottom of the Mariana Trench.

As a nuclear weapons expert, he was the only one on board who knew what to look for once they reached the bottom.

Marazzato was also the only person on board who had very specific instructions from the Pentagon on what was to be done if nuclear waste was identified.

He just hoped that he would have the strength to go through with it when the time came.

CHAPTER THIRTY-FIVE

INSIDE THE COMMAND CENTER ONBOARD the *Tahila*, Elise sat monitoring an array of screens, including those that tracked the health of the three submarine occupants, who wore wristbands that monitored their vital signs as they descended.

Matthew stepped down from the helm, looking over her shoulder at the monitors. "How's everyone doing down there?"

"Good, they've reached three thousand feet and for the most part their initial nerves have settled, but I'm still a little worried about James Marazzato."

"The Major?" Matthew raised his eyebrows. "That surprises me. I would have thought with his background and training, he wouldn't have any problems going down in the sub."

"It happens. Some of the toughest men out there panic inside a submarine." Elise made a half-shrug. "His heart rate, like the rest of them has been a little higher than normal—a common sign of fear, but unlike the rest of the crew, his appears to keep increasing. Any chance he suffers with claustrophobia and it wasn't picked up before now?"

Matthew grimaced. "Take it from me Elise; everyone suffers

with a certain amount of claustrophobia, no matter how many times they descend to the depths of the ocean. My bet, he's just a bit anxious being on board the seventh submersible to ever reach the bottom of the Mariana Trench. He'll settle."

"I hope you're right."

Next to her, Veyron, an engineer and world leader on submersibles sat, studying a set of monitors that observed all technical data coming from *Ursula*.

"How's our sub looking, Veyron?" Elise asked.

"She's looking good. All systems appear to be functioning normally. They're on track to have enough gas for life-support to continue for a total of five days."

"Very good."

Elise was happy with all that she saw, but despite it she could feel the sweat building on her forehead and a slight tingling sensation within her spine.

Something's not right.

She knew it was nothing more than a sixth sense, but had learned not to dismiss its value over the years.

Elise swept an array of navigational monitors, her eyes landing on the radar. It showed a single vessel, a fishing boat six miles to their east.

"Matthew, how long's that fishing boat been out there?" she asked.

"Nearly twenty minutes," Matthew replied.

"Where's it headed?"

"Nowhere. It's at a full stop."

Elise swallowed. "Ah crap."

"Why? What's wrong?"

"What's it doing out here?"

"Fishing I guess." Matthew shrugged his shoulders. "Why?"

"It's just a hunch," Elise said, but her heart started to race. "I need some headphones; I want to listen to the hydrophone myself."

Veyron passed her a spare pair.

"You won't hear much from the *Ursula* with that," Veyron said. "They're already too deep."

"I'm not interested in what they have to say — I want to know what our fishing friends are after and I'm willing to bet money it's not just fish."

Elise listened for less than ten seconds and then carefully removed her earphones, taking a digital print out of the ship's acoustics. Every ship made a unique sound. It didn't matter if the ship appeared identical, was built in the same shipyard by the same group of construction workers and engineers, somehow, they all came out with their own independent sound signature.

She copied the digital recording into the database, and clicked on match.

She watched the readout for the ship. It was in their database. She had a length of 354 feet, a beam of 56 feet, and a hull displacement of 5,763 tons. It was registered as the Russian Navy's Underwater Research vessel, the *Yantar* — but most people knew her primary purpose was maritime espionage.

Elise said, "They're trawling all right, but not for fish."

"What do you mean?" Matthew asked.

"I mean they almost certainly have their own hydrophones in the water, listening to what we're doing."

"Let's not be too quick to give the game away. We don't want an international crisis on our hands." Matthew said, setting his jaw firm. "We don't know exactly what their intentions are. They wouldn't be stupid enough to attack us this close to our Navy base on Guam, so let's wait and see what they want."

"All right," Elise said. "I'll send Sam a digital message."

Elise turned to the data log, which had an individual messaging system, like airline pilots used to communicate with engineers on the ground during their flights. She typed the words, SAM, WE HAVE GUESTS."

CHAPTER THIRTY-SIX

SAM REILLY GLANCED AT THE depth gauge.
They were approaching the 35,000-foot mark. He flicked on the external lights and switched off the autopilot, taking control of the submersible with the fine and adept movements of a handheld joystick.

The bathymetric imaging showed the seafloor racing up to greet them.

Sam leveled the submarine off at 35,500 feet.

The Mariana Trench is part of the Pacific Ring of Fire, a tectonically active region where plates are colliding with each other, causing subduction—a process whereby one plate dives beneath another—and transform faulting, where plates slide by one another. The old seafloor of the Pacific Plate is subducting beneath the eastern part of the Mariana Plate, causing the mantle to melt and magma to rise, feeding the active volcanoes of the Izu-Bonin-Mariana volcanic arc system.

West of the arc volcanoes is the back-arc, a zone of extensional tectonics that causes spreading in the overriding plate and forms new oceanic crust. As seawater percolates downward through the oceanic crust, it becomes superheated and chemical-rich, eventually getting so buoyant that it comes back out at the seafloor surface. When the super-hot vent fluid meets the very cold water of the deep sea, minerals that are carried in the fluid precipitate out of solution, forming spectacular vent chimneys. This chemical-rich vent fluid is also the source of life for much of the vent biota.

It was these chemical-rich vents that now flowed upward to greet them.

Ursula's LED beams shined down on their other-worldly environment, rich in its unique landscape. Large seamounts rose from the valley floor, like ancient buildings, intermingled with guyots—their flat-topped seamounts having been mysteriously sheered away. Dispersed between these, were row upon row of hydrothermal vents.

It was these vents that provided energy for the billions of strange marine creatures, known as extremophiles for their ability to survive in a world previously thought incapable of supporting life. The vents, like the creatures that inhabited them, were rich in their sheer diversity—there were black smokers filled with sulfide minerals, liquid carbon dioxide vents at the NW Eifuku volcano, and even craters erupting molten sulfur!

Thriving in these seemingly inhospitable environments, were throngs of organisms, including gastropods, mussels, tubeworms, galatheid crabs, and shrimp.

Sam maneuvered the submersible north, navigating through the rising seamounts. *Ursula's* propellers whirred as she moved forward at a leisurely three knots. The trench dropped off into a deeper valley, and Sam shifted the joystick forward, descending to follow the natural topography of the seabed as he went.

Sam's eyes swept the nearby landscape. He grinned. Up ahead were more than a hundred black smoker vents littering the seafloor like some sort of ancient burned out forest. Their black chimney-like structures rose upward some fifty feet above the seabed, emitting particles with high levels of sulfur-bearing minerals, or sulfides. They formed thousands of feet below the Earth's crust, where superheated water broke through.

Intermingled in this unique forest, were a series of white smokers that surprisingly coexisted in the same dense region of seafloor. While black smokers burned hotter, white smoker vents emitted lighter-hued minerals, such as those containing barium, calcium and silicon.

Sam glanced over his shoulder at his two guests. "What do you think of that?"

Dr. Smyth smiled, her eyes wide with awe. "I've never seen anything like it."

"I've read books about it," Major Marazzato said, "but it didn't come close to preparing me for the actual sight of being here."

"Yeah, it's something," Sam said, bringing the submersible to a stop, hovering just five feet back from a large hydrothermal vent.

His eyes swept the base of the vent, taking in the multitude of shrimp, mussels, and crabs that played in the superheated sulphur, a 680-degrees Fahrenheit toxic playground, where they consumed chemosynthetic bacteria for food.

Sam asked, "How's that for the food chain?"

Major Marazzato scrunched his face up tight. "I don't see what's eating what down here. Or is something larger simply boiling these creatures for dinner?"

Sam laughed. "Yeah, it's hard to tell. Particularly because most of the creatures there aren't following the normal direction of an ecological food chain."

Dr. Smyth shifted in her chair to get a better look. "So, what is eating what down there?"

Sam stared at the central burning tower of superheated water and chemicals. "Hydrothermal vent communities are able to sustain such vast amounts of life because vent organisms depend on chemosynthetic bacteria for food."

"Come again?" Major Marazzato frowned. "In English this time, Mr. Reilly."

"The water from the hydrothermal vent is rich in dissolved minerals and supports a large population of chemoautotrophic bacteria. These bacteria use sulfur compounds, particularly hydrogen sulfide, a chemical highly toxic to most known organisms, to produce organic material through the process of chemosynthesis."

"Like plants use sunlight to sustain the growth of green leafy foliage, which serves the basis of most organic food chains on the surface of Earth," Dr. Smyth suggested.

"Exactly. Only, down here, there is no sunlight. Not even any hint of creatures that once gained their nutrients from the sun. So instead, they rely on chemicals to directly synthesize their organic materials."

"But some of those creatures look like they're still eating the smaller ones," argued Dr. Smyth.

"That's right," Sam admitted. "Just because the food chain exists due to the chemical rich hydrothermal vents and the process of chemosynthesis, doesn't mean all the members of the food chain have to follow suit."

Marazzato smiled. "You mean the little guys eat the chemicals and the big guys eat the little guys who eat the chemicals?"

"Yeah, that's pretty much how it goes. The chemosynthetic bacteria grow into a thick mat which attracts other organisms, such as amphipods and copepods, which graze upon the bacteria directly. Larger organisms, such as snails, shrimp, crabs, tube worms, fish and octopuses form a food chain of predator and prey relationships with the primary consumers." Sam stared at the base of the vent. "The main families of organisms found around seafloor vents are annelids, pogonophorans, gastropods, and crustaceans, with large bivalves, vestimentiferan worms, and "eyeless" shrimp making up the bulk of non-microbial organisms. The bigger organisms such as fish and octopus sometimes get too close to the vents, whereupon they get burned and die. Like everywhere else on the planet, their decomposing bodies will be eaten by smaller, scavenger animals that lay in wait on the seabed surrounding the vents."

"What about the tubeworms?" Dr. Smyth asked. "They look like they're eating bacteria inside and outside the vents."

Sam shook his head. "Tubeworms do not eat. They have neither a mouth nor a stomach. Instead, billions of symbiotic bacteria living inside the tubeworms produce sugars from carbon dioxide, hydrogen sulfide, and oxygen."

Marazzato shook his head. "And I thought we had problems up on the surface. Talk about a different way of life."

Sam met each of his guest's eyes. "You two seen enough?"

"Yeah, we know these creatures, unique though they are, belong here," Dr. Smyth said. "But it's time to go see what that sphere is. Something I believe definitely doesn't belong here."

"All right, let's go."

Sam shifted the joystick to the right and the submersible darted round a particularly large hydrothermal vent.

Ursula followed the natural topography of the seafloor and stopped.

There, in front of them, was a completely flat region of land, some thousands of feet across. It was smooth and level, as though someone had come through the region with a bulldozer and leveled the entire seabed.

Major Marazzato raised his eyebrows. "What the hell is this place?"

Sam swallowed hard. "I have no idea; I was hoping you could tell me."

Marazzato shook his head. "Beats the hell out of me. We definitely didn't do this, if that's what you're asking. The US Military doesn't have anything that could level an area this large underwater. Hell, if I had to guess, it looks like this entire place has been intentionally leveled… or bulldozed."

"Or mined?" Sam suggested.

Marazzato paused, taking the question in seriously. "Yes, that's a strong possibility. Although I wouldn't have thought anyone had the technology to make mining materials at this depth viable."

"It might not be as impossible as it sounds," Sam said. "Many hydrothermal vents are rich in cobalt, gold, copper, and rare earth metals essential for electronic components. Recently, mineral exploration companies, driven by the elevated price activity in the base metals sector during the mid-2000s, have turned their attention to extraction of mineral resources from hydrothermal fields on the seafloor. Significant cost reductions are, in theory, possible."

"Sure, but at this depth?"

"It's unlikely, but far from science fiction." Sam made a half-shrug. "Maybe they're using an entirely different process to extract the minerals. Could a nuclear bomb have been detonated here?"

Dr. Smyth shook her head. "No. It's too flat. The blast radius would sweep downward as well as outward, meaning there would be some signs of the damage to the seabed, but instead, the entire region looks unnaturally flat."

Ursula's propellers continued to whine as they headed toward the center of the flattened mass, where no hydrothermal vents, seamounts, or guyots, existed anymore — leaving a blank scar on the seabed, like a crater in the moon.

Nearly a mile in, Sam brought the submersible to a complete standstill.

There in front of them, was a perfect sphere, with a diameter of five hundred feet.

It was made of obsidian.

And no light either penetrated it or was released from within.

"Holy shit!" Sam swore, "Elise, are you getting this topside?"

There was no answer.

Because, next to him, Major James Marazzato had just cut through the communication's cable.

CHAPTER THIRTY-SEVEN

Phang Nga Bay, Thailand

THE WIND BLEW KATALE'S KABANG at a leisurely four knots across the Phang Nga Bay, heading southwest toward Phuket. He swiftly sailed past the first of many limestone cliffs and rock formations that towered high above the blue-green cyan waters, colorful coral reefs, and white sandy beaches.

His father was missing.

That on its own could have meant any number of things had happened. He might be traveling farther off shore in search of fish, or he might be dead. Either way, there was nothing Katale could do about it.

But now, others from his flotilla had gone missing.

One by one, all males from his flotilla had disappeared.

Unlike his father, who still truly believed that the good and evil sea spirits ruled their destiny, and that nothing could be done to influence one's life, Katale had learned to speak English, and had taken a job guiding tourists to visit his community. Over the past two years, he'd learned just how much farther the world extended outside the Mergui Archipelago.

His young mind had absorbed the information like a sponge. He'd taken the time to learn to read. It was difficult, and so far, he'd only progressed to the size books that a small child might consume, but already it had taught him things about the world.

It was indeed filled with good and evil.

But those spirits weren't just found beneath the sea. People were good and evil. Even non-people, something called countries, and powerful organizations that ruled people could be good and evil. The Myanmar Navy sometimes helped his people, while at other times, its people stole from them, and burned their boats.

When his father first disappeared, he thought it could have been caused by any number of unfortunate events that went hand in hand with being Moken. But when every one of his father's friends disappeared after his father had gone out to gather the sea gypsies in order to determine what to do about the strange glass dome beneath the seabed. Katale became certain the events were related.

He thought of the strange drawing on the side of the canister the man was carrying inside the dome. There was something about it that was important. He'd shown the drawing to everyone he knew, but no one could tell him what it meant.

That's why he was heading to Phang Nga Bay.

He was looking for a Thai man named Eamon, who currently had a job paddling kayaks for tourists through the Phang Nga Bay's limestone caves and lagoons. Eamon's Thai name translated to, *Rich Guardian*. And in many ways, that was what the man had become to Katale. Eamon had once traveled to America, and knew more about people and the world than any other person alive. If anyone could help him find his father and what had happened to the older men of his flotilla, it would be Eamon.

He pulled out of the wind, heading into the nearby lee of the white cliffs, where a couple large sea eagles soared on the thermals. At the base of the cliffs, a series of tourist boats were tied up together—all traditional Thai long-tails with their most defining feature being that of a car engine mounted on an inboard turret-like pole that could rotate through 180 degrees, allowing steering by thrust vectoring.

Katale greeted the first pilot he spotted. "Hello."

The man smiled, eying him cautiously. "Hello."

"Do you know where Eamon is working today?"

The stranger shook his head, as if to say he didn't know him.

"Please. I just need to talk to him."

The man shrugged. "I don't know him."

Katale turned to keep heading south along the bay, but a pilot from a long-tailed boat shouted, "Eamon's working at Koh Phanak."

"Thank you."

Katale rowed out into the wind and opened his square sail of woven pandanus leaves. It unfurled and caught the wind, pulling him swiftly toward Koh Phanak.

By midday, he had reached it.

The entire region was littered with startling limestone karsts. Tunnels, funnels, channels, and caves all honeycombed the island.

He checked the row of long-tail boats, but no one could point him in the direction of his friend. He tied his kabang to an overhanging piece of limestone, and waited. If Eamon was taking tourists into the cave system, he would have to come out through the main cavern.

An hour went by. Most tourists in their inflatable kayaks returned from their day trips, but Katale didn't spot his friend.

A big powerboat with twin outboard engines roared across the bay heading toward him. Its pilot brought the engines to an idle, and the boat meandered toward the cave system, before pulling up alongside his kabang.

The man had very pale skin and blond hair. He stared at Katale, scrutinizing him. "Are you Katale?"

Katale stood up. "Yes?"

"Is your father a Moken leader from the North-Wind flotilla?"

Katale's eyes beamed wide. "Do you know my father?"

"Know him?" The man's evil eyes narrowed, and a vicious, thin-lipped smile tortured the villainous face with a grin. "Hell, I was the guy who shot him!"

Katale didn't have a chance to respond.

The stranger withdrew a handgun and fired directly at him.

Katale dived into the green water beneath the boat. He swam straight down, disappearing into the murky waters at the cavern's opening. Shots ripped through the water above, losing their momentum, and falling aimlessly beside him.

He kicked hard, swimming beneath the lip of the overhanging cavern, which extended deep into the water, before swimming up the other side.

Katale took in a deep breath.

Outside the cavern someone shouted, "He's still alive. Go after him!"

"Are you kidding me, the tide's rising, we'll drown!" came someone's reply.

The man said, "Go after him, or they will make you wish you'd drowned."

Katale kept swimming deeper into the karst passageway. At low tide tourists were taken into these tunnels in kayaks by the droves. At high tide the entire labyrinth of underground passageways, drainage systems, and sinkholes were flooded through.

He kicked his feet and swam harder.

The tunnel was nearly three hundred feet long. If it wasn't quite high tide yet, he would make it. If it was, then there was nothing he could do about it. There was no way even he could hold his breath that long.

He swam through the next passageway, which opened up to a wider tunnel. Green stalactites had formed into organic sculptures and white stalagmites appeared ghost-like through the gloom. Above, he heard the flutter of nocturnal wings, as bats adjusted their positions.

Katale kept moving. There wasn't much time. Behind him, he heard the sound of labored breathing and fear. It brought a smile to his lips. At least his pursuers weren't going to have a good time of it. There was every chance that they, too, would drown with him.

The thought gave him confidence.

If he was going to die, so be it that the gods should take his attackers with him.

The limestone ceiling tapered downward, progressively reducing the remaining chamber of air, until it disappeared completely.

Katale took a couple deep breaths, and dived underneath.

The narrow passageway was now pitch dark, meaning he needed to run his hands along the slimy submerged walls to ensure he kept moving in the right direction. He kicked with his legs and the muscles in his chest burned, begging him to take another breath.

Light appeared up ahead, and he kicked harder, until the passageway opened up into a large hong—the remains of an ancient sinkhole.

Katale took another deep breath, followed by several more, as he caught his wind. The place was surrounded by near vertical white cliffs, upon which a thick jungle of dense vegetation clung and wild macaque crab-eating monkeys played.

Standing alone in the middle of the hong was a tall man—one of the biggest men he'd ever seen—and a beautiful woman with short brown hair. The two appeared to have been in the process of an intimate kiss, when they were startled by the intrusion.

The woman was the first to notice him. She smiled. It was impish and mischievous. Like she was caught, but it didn't matter, because she would do it again if she was given the chance. She said, "Hi there."

Katale smiled back. "Hello."

His eyes darted toward the entrance.

The tide had well and truly now come in, and the tunnels inside were being quickly flooded. They were now trapped on the inside of the hong — safe until the tide fell — whereupon his enemies would now have him trapped.

He swallowed hard at the thought.

But he didn't have to wait. Instead, a man surfaced five or so feet away from him.

The man, noticing the two strangers enjoying their tranquility at the center of the hong, shot at them.

The shots sprayed the shallow water.

And both the girl and man dived out of the way, their heads disappearing into the shallow water.

Their attacker turned and spotted Katale, firing the last of his rounds at him. He dived under the water and tried to swim across the hong, taking refuge on the opposite side.

Katale stared at his attacker, who loaded another magazine into his weapon.

Where did the two strangers go?

Had they been shot dead?

Katale's eyes darted across the water, searching for a place to hide or take refuge. His attacker cocked his submachinegun, drawing the first round from his magazine.

Katale held his breath, waiting for the first shot to pierce his flesh.

His attacker pulled the trigger.

Katale heard the loud report of the shot as it echoed through the surrounding cliffs.

And the big guy emerged from beneath the shallow water, lifting the man up by his feet. The attacker fell backward. He yanked at the submachinegun's trigger, sending a sharp burst of shots scattering across the white limestone walls.

A moment later, the woman appeared behind the attacker. She moved with a warrior's speed, and the precision of an athlete, as she sliced a small razorblade across their attacker's throat.

The weapon fell, and the man tried desperately to stem the bleeding with both his hands. But it was a losing battle. His carotid artery had been severed in one clean slice. The man's eyes widened in terror, before rolling in the back of his head.

The woman waited a full minute, and then discarded the dead body.

She turned to face Katale. "You want to tell me what that was all about?"

CHAPTER THIRTY-EIGHT

The Lost World, Hong-Koh Phanak, Thailand

THE LIFE-GIVING HUMIDITY OF the tropics allowed plants to take hold and thrive in any horizontal, and many vertical, surfaces. As this dense vegetation inevitably dies and rots, it forms more soil on which new life flourishes. Rainwater percolates through the slowly building soil and through the limestone, creating holes as it reaches sea level. Eventually, the soil becomes too heavy for the pitted rock, and sinkholes come crashing through to form a hong—a lost world, within a limestone mountain, a secret lagoon.

The walled lagoon was covered by the most brilliant greenery, where monkeys had played on the vines that ran hundreds of feet into the air, and birds had chirped, insects thrummed, and small fish splashed in the shallow water.

There was only silence after the gunfire.

Tom glanced at their attacker, lying dead in the water, surrounded by an expanding pool of blood. He didn't need to get any closer to make certain the threat had been eliminated.

Genevieve didn't make mistakes. She didn't care who their attacker was, where he'd come from, or who he was with. The man had shot at them, and therefore needed to be taken out. Other questions could be asked and answered later.

Tom's eyes darted toward the small, dark-skinned boy, whose face was set aghast, in abject horror, his hands shaking uncontrollably. "You okay, kid?"

The kid nodded. His mouth opened, but he didn't speak. Instead the kid's eyes kept flicking between the dead man and the flooded entrance to the now submerged passageway.

"What is it?" Tom asked, his eyes narrowing. "Are there more people coming for you?"

The kid nodded.

"How many?"

"I don't know," the kid replied. "They came on a big power boat. There might have been three… maybe four men."

"Were they all carrying weapons," Genevieve asked, her mind racing toward the practicality of shutting down any immediate threat.

"I don't know. They all kept shooting at me."

Genevieve picked up the man's weapon. "It's a Russian Vityaz closed-bolt submachinegun." Her lips formed into a broad grin, as she casually examined the weapon, as an art-dealer might examine a rare painting. "My father trained me on the very same type of weapon when I was a child."

Tom made a half-grin. "Of course he did, darling. What more could the head of the Russian Mafia want for his daughter?"

She raised her trimmed eyebrows. "What indeed?"

Genevieve unclipped the magazine. It was empty. She searched the man's body for another magazine, but came up short. "We're out of luck."

Tom turned to the young boy, who seemed more frightened now having watched Genevieve work the submachinegun like a deadly mercenary, than he had a minute ago.

Tom said, "I'm Tom and you have Genevieve over there to thank for saving your life."

The kid's eyes darted from Genevieve to Tom, tracing the white cliffs of the surrounding lagoon, before landing back reluctantly on Tom. "My name's Katale. Thank you both for saving my life."

Tom said, "You're welcome."

"Any time," Genevieve said, as she cleaned her razor blade on the dead man's jacket shirt. "Why were they chasing you?"

"I don't know..."

Genevieve looked incredulous. "Four men nearly drowned trying to kill you, and you have no idea why?"

"No. Not really..." Katale paused, swallowing hard. "I think I might know what this is all about, but none of it makes sense. You will definitely think I'm crazy."

"Try us," Tom suggested.

"Two weeks ago, I was diving on an outer reef near Horse Shoe Island, looking for lobster for my flotilla."

A grin formed on Tom's mouth. "You're Moken?"

"Yes."

"I didn't think Moken had anything to do with outsiders?" Tom said. "You speak English very well."

"Thank you. Most Moken are traditionalists. We live as hunter gatherers, and believe the bountiful sea will provide for us. But times are changing whether we like it or not. The Thai and Myanmar governments are encroaching on our fishing waters, and have taken to constricting our movement on islands that have traditionally been used by my people. Two years ago, much to my father's displeasure, I took a job guiding tourists through our islands, villages, and flotillas. In that time I soon discovered that the world is a much bigger place than I could have ever imagined."

Tom said, "Welcome to the bigger world. Is that how you ended tied up with... what? The Russian mafia?"

"I don't know. Like I said before, I don't really understand what's happened, and I very much doubt you'll believe me when I tell you."

Tom said, "Try us. Take us back to two weeks ago, when you were diving for lobster."

Katale closed his eyes, thinking about the past. "Okay. The fishing was poor. Something had spooked the fish, causing them to disappear. It happens. Not often, but it does. The good news is, when the fish disappear, the crayfish come out of their hiding places from beneath the rocky reef, to go in search of food."

"So you went crayfish gathering instead?"

"Yeah." Katale nodded. "Only I didn't find any crayfish either. So I kept going farther out. I was just about to turn back when I spotted it."

"What?"

"Some sort of glittering light, reflecting off the seafloor. I thought it was gold."

"I didn't know Moken people had any interest in material things... something about most possessions slowing you down. Did I get that wrong?"

"No. We don't in general. But gold is different."

Tom laughed. "Gold is always coveted by man."

"No. It's not what you think. The gold attracts fish with its ability to reflect light, meaning we can use it to catch fish. We have little use for most possessions, but our fishing tools are our lifelines, so yes, those possessions we love and cherish more than any child would his toys."

Tom said, "Okay, so you dived down to retrieve the gold..."

"But it wasn't gold."

"What was it?"

"That's the crazy part."

Tom urged him, "Go on. What was it?"

"A dome. A glass dome of some sort. The recent changes in

weather must have shifted some of the sand which had kept it well covered and hidden for many years."

"But what was it?"

"I don't know. A glass dome of some kind. It was big enough that a fully-grown man could easily walk around inside."

Tom's eyes narrowed. "You're telling me someone was alive inside?"

"Yes. More than that. He was moving around. He seemed disturbed when he saw me, as though he'd been caught out doing something bad."

"What was he doing?"

"He was moving something. A large canister. There were lots of them down there."

Tom breathed heavily, his heart racing at the news. "Do you know what was inside the canister?"

Katale shook his head. "No. But it had a strange marking over it."

"What was the marking?"

"I don't know," Katale replied, "but I can draw it for you."

Tom watched as the kid took a stone and started to scratch it into the soft limestone wall.

Katale scratched a circle with a smaller circle in the middle of it. Between the two circles, he drew three separate triangles, making the shape of a trefoil.

The muscles around Tom's jaw tightened. "Let me guess, it was colored yellow?"

Katale nodded, "How did you know?"

Tom swallowed down the fear that rose in his throat like bile. "Because that's one of the most recognizable symbols in the world. It's an international warning that nuclear radiation is nearby."

Genevieve said, "I guess that explains why someone was out to kill you."

"Yeah, if ever there was a motive for killing off an entire tribe, there's one." Tom met the kid's eye. He looked like he was close to tears. "We'd better get going. I think you'd better come with us."

"Where? There's no way out and we're trapped."

Tom shook his head. "There's a dry limestone passageway that takes us out to the opposite side of the island. We have a float plane waiting for us. What do you say? Do you want to make whoever's responsible pay for what they've done?"

Katale looked at him, and said, "Hell yes."

CHAPTER THIRTY-NINE

Office of the Chairman of the Joint Chiefs of Staff, Pentagon

GENERAL LOUIS C. PAINTER, THE chairman of the Joint Chiefs of Staff looked at the single photograph of the obsidian sphere on his table.

He sighed heavily and handed it to the Senator seated across from him.

The Senator glanced at the photo. His brow furrowed. "Where was this taken?"

"At the bottom of the Mariana Trench. Two hours ago."

The Senator shook his head in dismay. "How did they even find it after all these years?"

"There was some sort of shipping disaster. A submarine volcano erupted, evidently bringing the sphere's nuclear waste to the surface. A wealthy Silicon Valley entrepreneur and his crew died. There was an investigation."

The Senator's eyes narrowed. "And you let them keep going?"

General painter's countenance was set firm. "Hell, you think I had any idea what they were going to find down there?"

"Who's doing the investigation?"

"Sam Reilly."

That brought silence.

The Senator thought about that for a moment, as he ran his hands across his forehead. "Quick, you've got to stop their dive."

General Painter crossed his arms. "I can't. It's already done. They're down there now."

"Ah crap. You know what's going to happen."

Painter said, "We always knew our past would come back to haunt us sometime. I suppose we should be thankful it took this long."

"Yes. The question is, now what are we going to do about it?"

"Nothing. I have an agent traveling there now to inspect the site. With any luck, nothing will be left to incriminate us."

"And what if someone's still alive?"

"From the original crew of Habitat Zero? You've got to be kidding, that's gotta be what… at least seventy years old!"

The senator said, "They'll remember what we did to them. And they're not going to be happy. Hell, the world won't be happy with what we've done."

General Painter's lips hardened into a straight line. "Hey, you and I didn't start this shit-fight."

"You think the world is going to care about who started this? Or do you think they're going to remember who failed to stop it?"

General Painter said, "It's all right. If someone's still alive down there, my agent will know what to do. They won't be alive for much longer…"

CHAPTER FORTY

The Obsidian Sphere

SAM REILLY GRIPPED THE SUBMARINE'S joystick trying to regain control of *Ursula*.

He shifted it all the way backward and then all the way forward but nothing happened. He flicked it to the right, but the submarine didn't respond. Instead, the ship continued to slowly sink toward the artificially leveled seabed below.

Breathing hard, he fought with the buoyancy controls, trying to stabilize the vessel. He glanced at the bathymetric depth sounder, which showed the distance between the bottom of the submarine and the seabed below.

Forty-feet.

Dr. Smyth said, "What's happening."

Sam ran his hands across a series of emergency ballast tanks, flicking switches that were designed to send them racing toward the surface. "I don't know. I've lost all controls."

Thirty-feet.

They continued toward the seabed.

Twenty-feet.

Ten-feet.

"Hold on!" Sam said. "This is going to be a rough landing."

Five-feet.

Ursula's twin pontoons crashed lightly into the gray mud of the seabed, and the submarine came to rest.

The mud settled in silence.

Major James Marazzato said, "What the hell went wrong?"

Sam took a slow, purposefully deep breath in and exhaled. "When you severed the communications feed to the surface, you sliced through the main controls module."

"Meaning?"

"It means that I no longer have any control over the submarine's controls. AKA — we're now sitting ducks."

"We're trapped, here?" Marazzato shifted uncomfortably on his seat, his eyes staring at the borosilicate dome, as if searching for fine cracks to form. "Stranded on the bottom of the world's deepest seabed!"

Sam's lips twisted into malevolent pleasure, as fear crossed Marazzato's face. "Yes. We're stranded here because you thought it was a good idea to sever the communications cable with the surface. What the hell did you think you were doing?"

Marazzato opened his mouth to speak, mumbling something inaudible.

Sam said, "What? If we're going to die down here, you might as well tell me what for?"

"I needed to make sure no one on the surface could see this video footage." Marazzato placed the palms of his hands upward. "Don't you see how important it is to protect this? It needs to be safeguarded."

"How protected do you think it's going to be when we don't return to the surface?" Sam asked. "And the US Navy, along with major media outlets, send an armada out here to find the truth?"

Major Marazzato said, "I'm sorry."

Dr. Smyth said, "What about the emergency ballast system? I thought the dome capsule could be released in an emergency?"

"It should, but it didn't work."

"Why not?" she asked.

"I don't know. I tried the manual latch. There is something about the pressure that the engineers didn't quite understand. It's not their fault; no one has really experimented at this depth."

"So we're really trapped here?"

Sam nodded. "For the time being at least."

"Until when?" Marazzato asked.

"In five days the sodium crystal anodes on the twin pontoons will dissolve, releasing the heavy lead ballast weights. When that happens, we'll be on a one way trip to the surface." Sam made an uncomfortable grin. "That is, of course, on the assumption that the system doesn't have any unexpected faults."

CHAPTER FORTY-ONE

THE TEMPERATURE IN THE SUBMARINE dropped quickly.

The hours ticked by slowly.

Boredom struck first, followed by hunger. They had survival rations, but those needed to be withheld for as long as possible. Sam checked the computer, making certain that the life support and gas supplies were going to make it.

Dr. Smyth took photos of the sphere using a hand-held digital camera.

"Hey, you can't do that!" Major Marazzato tried to take the camera from her. "This falls under the government's Secrecy Act."

"What are you talking about?" Dr. Smyth held the camera solid. "I was sent here to determine if someone was illegally dumping nuclear waste."

"Yeah, well, we've already discovered that the nuclear waste isn't coming from wherever we thought it might have been. It's clearly surrounding the sphere. That's alien technology. It should be kept secret until the Navy can send an extraction team to secure it. We're going to need to protect it."

"How do you think that will work?" Sam said. "The sphere has a diameter of five hundred feet. We don't have the technology to secure it, let alone bring it to the surface."

"That's for the engineers to work out, Mr. Reilly. My job is to protect the secret until they can retrieve it."

Dr. Smyth gripped her camera. "And my job is to make sure some rogue nuclear nation isn't about to poison the ocean with nuclear waste."

Sam intervened. "We've all come here to work out what's going on. If that means the sphere is responsible for the leaking nuclear waste, then so be it. If it's alien technology, or something made by one of our enemies, the Department of Defense will take over all responsibility after we get to the surface and brief the Secretary of Defense. Until then, Major Marazzato, I suggest you allow Dr. Smyth to do her job."

Dr. Smyth said, "Thank you, Mr. Reilly."

Sam turned his attention to the sphere. On closer inspection, it wasn't a perfect sphere. It was shaped evenly, but what appeared like a smooth globe of obsidian had some imperfections in the form of deep recesses and crevasses.

He focused on a large one near the bottom of the sphere. There was something familiar about it. Something he couldn't quite put his finger on. The recess looked like something he'd seen on a nuclear submarine.

To Dr. Smyth, he said, "Can you get a close-up picture of that opening, for me please?"

"Sure. I'll see what I can get." Dr. Smyth took a couple photos, zooming in as close as she could to the opening. She handed him the camera, "See if you can make anything of it."

Sam stared at the image. His mouth opened in shock.

Major Marazzato glanced at him, "What is it? What do you see?"

Sam grimaced, fixing his gaze directly on the major. "James, we're trapped on the bottom of the world's deepest ocean, in a bubble not much bigger than the iron coffin of the last generation's deep-sea divers. In all likelihood, there's a very good chance we're not going to make it to the surface again. You understand that, don't you?"

Major Marazzato nodded. "Yes I do."

"Good." Sam met his eye. "That being the case, can you answer me something honestly?"

"Shoot," Marazzato said.

Sam expelled a deep breath. "Is the sphere one of ours?"

Marazzato held his breath. "Of course not!"

"Are you sure?"

"Good God! Do you think we'd have even been allowed to dive if the sphere was our technology? Hell, the Pentagon wouldn't have even let you investigate the *Carpe Diem* if it was going to lead you to their own secret technology."

"Are you sure?"

"Of course I'm sure. Whoever that craft belongs to — if they are still alive — they've won the game. It's not a game changer — its game over for the rest of us." Marazzato balled his fists, as though he might actually win that sort of fight trapped inside a submarine on the seafloor. "Why are you so certain it's one of ours?"

Sam turned the camera around so that all three of them could see the image clearly. It depicted an opening into the sphere. Despite its massive size, the opening was very similar to the lockout trunk of a nuclear submarine.

And at the bottom right hand corner, painted onto the hull, was the flag of the United States of America.

CHAPTER FORTY-TWO

"DAMMIT MAJOR MARAZZATO!" SAM SAID, "How long have you known that this was down here?"

Marazzato bit his lower lip. He met Sam's eye, and then expelled a deep breath. "Look. I found out about it forty-eight hours ago."

"They knew about it and yet they sent us here anyway?"

He nodded without saying anything.

Sam asked, "Why?"

"Because they didn't really believe it was true."

"What was true?"

"That the sphere really existed."

Sam tried to blink the confusion out of his eyes. "What are you talking about? They either knew about it or they didn't."

Marazzato frowned. "I'm afraid it's not quite that simple."

"Bullshit!" Sam slammed his fist on the control panel in front of him. "It exactly that simple. We're going to die down here because of you, so I think it's fair that you at least let me know why?"

Marazzato nodded, almost accepting that it was a reasonable idea. "They've known about the sphere since the sixties."

Sam's brow furrowed. "The sixties?"

Marazzato took a deep breath. "Middle of the cold war they found it floating in the Atlantic Ocean twenty miles off the coast of Chesapeake Bay."

"A giant sphere with a diameter of a thousand feet washes up that close to Washington and no one suspects an attack?"

Marazzato raised the palms of his hands. "No. They had serious doubts it had come from the Soviets."

"Really? Haven't they ever heard of a Trojan Horse?"

"Apparently not." Marazzato handed Sam the camera back. "And besides, I believe this already answers the question of who built it. The question now is, when was it built?"

Sam arched his eyebrow. "What are you saying?"

"I'm saying that we don't currently have the technology to build something like the sphere today. Certainly nothing in the US Navy. You said yourself that the dome that's keeping the three of us alive is the cutting edge of deep water submersible technology, and it only has a diameter of under ten feet. Do you really believe we have the technology to build something as grand as the sphere?"

"So if the US Navy didn't build it, who did?"

"Not who. We know it was built by us. That's not in dispute. The door even has our logo."

Sam persisted. "But you're saying the US Navy didn't build it?"

Major Marazzato sighed heavily. "No. I'm saying the US Navy hasn't built it yet."

CHAPTER FORTY-THREE

"YOU SERIOUSLY THINK IT'S COME from the future?" Sam asked, without even trying to suppress his skepticism.

Major Marazzato shrugged. "You got a better explanation?"

"Yeah, I do," Dr. Smyth said.

Sam grinned. "Well, don't keep us all waiting in suspense, Dr. Smyth."

"All right," Dr. Smyth said. "I think it's some sort of secret weapon being developed by DARPA."

Sam considered that for a moment. DARPA stood for the Defense Advanced Research Projects Agency, an agency of the United States Department of Defense. They specialized in high tech defense research projects, many of them highly clandestine.

"It's a possibility. Unlikely, but always possible."

Marazzato shook his head, defiantly. "There's no way they could build a structure of that magnitude to survive the crushing pressure of the sea at this depth. No way!"

"Maybe it wasn't supposed to end up down here at all?" Dr. Smyth suggested. "Think about this for a moment. What if they were towing it somewhere and somewhere in the process, they lost control of the sphere. Or maybe it was on the surface and then sunk."

Marazzato said, "That still doesn't explain how it could survive the crushing pressure at this depth."

"Sure, but what if these doors lead all the way through the sphere, meaning that by now it's filled with water, equalizing the pressure inside and outside of the sphere?"

Sam gave that some thought. "In that case, the sphere would have no pressure difference to withstand. Yeah, it's physically possible. Certainly, a more likely scenario than a time traveling weapon built by us from the future."

"I'm not buying it," Marazzato said, emphatically.

Sam shrugged. "It doesn't matter. We won't be guessing much longer."

"Why?" Marazzato asked.

But nobody answered him.

Because, a door opened from within the massive lockout trunk inside the sphere. A giant truck drove out the door on stainless steel caterpillar tracks. A single borosilicate dome covered the machine's single occupant. The machine had two glowing headlights at the front, that looked like giant bug eyes. Positioned at the front of the machine was a large suction dredge cutter head, and a large storage container at the back.

"Holy shit!" Sam whispered. "Someone's worked out how to mine at 36,000 feet."

The driver met Sam's eyes.

And a moment later, the deep-sea mining machine turned sharply, heading straight toward them.

CHAPTER FORTY-FOUR

On Board *Tahila*, South of Guam

ELISE OPENED THE ENCRYPTED EMAIL.

It was from the Secretary of Defense, and had passed through a series of proxy-servers, designed to wheedle out any signs of tampering or eavesdropping viruses. She went through a series of standard checks to ascertain that the email was in fact legitimate and then clicked open.

A single page of words appeared.

The words were little more than gibberish. In addition to its array of digitally secure communication systems, the email retained a unique unbreakable code to be used for open communication. This one relied on a secret key cryptography to obscure its meaning. This type of code was a variation of the one-time pad—the only truly unbreakable code in theory. To decode the message, a listener had to have both the book and the key. Only in this case, it wasn't just a book, but a complete works of books.

Elise opened a second document on her laptop.

This one contained a digital copy of all of the classic works of Charles Dickens. Elise had very little direct communications with the Secretary of Defense, but when they did communicate it was vitally important as it needed to be secure.

Traditionally, secret key cryptography employs a single key for both encryption and decryption. In this case, a message was sent by the Secretary of Defense using the key to encrypt the plaintext and send the ciphertext to the receiver. The receiver applies the same key to decrypt the message and recover the plaintext.

Because a single key is used for both functions, secret key cryptography is also called symmetric encryption. When using a cipher, the original information is known as plaintext and the encrypted form as ciphertext. The ciphertext message contains all the information of the plaintext message—yet isn't in a format readable by human or computer without the proper mechanism to decrypt it.

Elise opened both the email document and the digital copy of Charles Dickens's complete, unabridged, works.

She scanned the email, ignoring all letters, and searching for individual numbers only. They were scattered throughout the document.

She collected them and placed them together to form a date—1854.

Elise then opened the table of contents, listing release dates of all of Charles Dickens's books. Her eyes stopped on the only one released that year.

Hard Times, by Charles Dickens—1854

The book focused on an unsympathetic look upon utilitarianism—an ethical theory that determines right from wrong by focusing on outcomes. It is a form of consequentialism. Utilitarianism holds that the most ethical choice is the one that will produce the greatest good for the greatest number

Elise smiled, and wondered if the Secretary of Defense was

hinting at something else to her.

She made a note, and then continued to decipher the code, by opening the document containing the book, *Hard Times*. She withdrew the key to the code from her pocket. Today was December 3 — thus she had to add the year, ignoring the first two digits, to the day's date. So, 3 and 18 made 21. She then opened the book to page twenty-one. December was the 12th month, so every 12th letter on the page would be discounted.

Using the key, she then went through the painfully slow process of deciphering the code until the series of individual letters made a recognizable series of words.

In this case, those words provided a link to a G-mail account and a password to access it. The account would have been set up just before the Secretary of Defense had sent the original message.

Elise opened up the email address and downloaded the single email sitting in the draft box.

Inside were a series of photographs taken from old Ivy League University graduation ceremonies dated 1961.

There were several black and white photographs. Each one depicting the graduating class from various Ivy League Universities. She ran her eyes across the university names — Harvard, Princeton, Yale, Brown, Dartmouth, they were all there. The best educations that old money could buy. Each photo had somewhere between twenty to fifty people, all with their matching names at the bottom in an index. A few faces, as many as five or six per photograph had been circled with a red pen. There was just one photograph that didn't depict a graduating class. This one, appeared to be of an ocean. The photo itself was of poor quality, but seemed to delineate some sort of dark sphere floating on the surface.

Elise put the photos in a document and then read the email.

The truth needs to come out. Search the names, and pull the strings. Only you can put this all together.

And break the code to Habitat Zero.

CHAPTER FORTY-FIVE

Office of the Chairman of the Joint Chiefs of Staff–Pentagon

GENERAL PAINTER PICKED UP THE phone.

He had been expecting the call. It was going to go badly, he knew that now, but sometimes it was better to deal with the most painful duties first.

This one came from a secure line, direct from the center of the maze within the 8th Continent.

"General Painter, Chairman of the Joint Chiefs of Staff, speaking," he said, using his full title.

"Painter," the man on the other side of the line replied, ignoring it. "We had a deal."

"With my predecessor, not me."

"All the same, a deal's a deal, and you must come through with it."

General Painter swallowed hard. "It was nearly seventy years ago. Hell, it was before I was born. You can't seriously believe I'm going to go through with it now."

"Seventy years isn't that long really... just a blink of an eye when you live as long as we do."

"Yeah, lucky you. I'm still not going through with it."

"But you have to. The natives have revolted against me in the 8th Continent. You need to fulfill your part of the bargain. I'm a damned prisoner in my own home."

"That's not my problem. It goes to show you can't suppress your people to remain subservient forever."

"What do you expect me to do? If I stay here, they will kill me!"

"From what I hear, the Master Builders are a dying race. Maybe it's time for you to join the rest of your people."

"After all these years, are you really going to turn your back on the covenant that John F. Kennedy signed?"

"Yeah. Why not? An alliance is only useful when both parties have something to gain—and right now, you're shit out of luck."

The man laughed. "Do you think we've survived in the shadows for thousands of years out of luck? You think it ends like this?"

"I don't see how you have any real choice. Your time is over. What other card do you have left to play?"

"I could always give it to the Russians?"

"You wouldn't dare!"

"If we offered you a deal in the sixties, why wouldn't we offer one to the Russians?"

CHAPTER FORTY-SIX

On Board *Tahila,* South of Guam

THE GENTLE SWELL GREW OVERNIGHT, and the crew of the *Tahila* awoke to large rolling waves. The wind picked up. The *Tahila* rode the swell with ease, but even she would struggle to maintain her position when the full brunt of a category five cyclone reached them.

Elise continued to search through the names of all the faces.

They read like a horror story. Something that Stephen King would write, some sort of bad luck tale, in which an entire group of graduates died, one after the other in simultaneous, seemingly unrelated events, tied together by an invisible string of bad luck within a year after graduating. Everyone of them had been the best in their field. Some had been engineers, doctors, scientists, biologists, all had been extraordinary in their own right.

She had searched every one of the names down.

There were thirty in total. All men. All now dead.

Some had died from car accidents. It was common in the

sixties. No seatbelts, and everyone drove intoxicated. One drowned. Three had hired a small plane to fly to Texas together for a conference on engineering. On the way, the plane got into trouble and crashed, leaving no survivors. Another was struck by lightning.

The list went on.

It would have been the basis of a true horror story.

If she believed any of it.

The wives disappeared, too. Every one of them. They went to visit their relatives, they traveled overseas, and one way or another, they all disappeared.

Elise took the first face and ran it through a database of newspapers, social media, politicians, scientists, and athletes using facial recognition software.

It came up with nothing.

She then inserted the entire set of faces into the program and pressed run.

The clock on her program indicated that it would take two hours to complete the search.

She stood up and stretched her legs.

Overhead, she heard the sound of a military helicopter hovering. It took off again a few minutes later, less three passengers.

Tom, Genevieve, and a young boy came down from the helipad.

Elise said, "Welcome back. How was your vacation?"

"Good," Tom said, "But it turns out the Russians look like they are illegally burying nuclear waste beneath the waters of the Andaman Sea off the coast of Myanmar."

"This is Katale by the way. He's going to show us exactly where it's being buried. He's going to be staying with us for a while, until we can investigate what's happening and bring it all out in the open."

Elise said, "Pleased to meet you, Katale."

"Thank you," Katale replied, his eyes searching the command center of the Tahila, as though it was some sort of gift from the Sea Gods.

Genevieve said, "Come with me Katale, I'll show you around."

As they left, Tom asked, "Any news from the submersible?"

Elise shook her head. "Not since its umbilical line was severed twelve hours ago."

Matthew stepped into the room. "Welcome back, Tom. Just in time, we're going to need to head off soon if we're to outrun this cyclone."

Tom's face hardened. "We're not waiting for Sam?"

"No," Matthew said. "It will be too risky. Sam knows about the cyclone. He'll wait on the bottom until this thing passes."

"What about the *Yantar?*" Tom asked. "Any news about what it's still doing here?"

"Spying I guess," Elise said. "What other use does a Russian spy vessel serve? You saw that sphere. It looks almost like a spacecraft. No wonder the Russians are interested."

Tom said, "Sure, but that doesn't answer the question, how the Russians knew about it."

"Knew about it?" Elise asked. "What are you talking about? The *Yantar* was probably simply here to track the *Tahila*, nothing more."

"I don't think so. It's too unlikely." Tom looked over at the Russian vessel on the horizon. "There are too many coincidences between this sphere and the nuclear waste dump beneath the Andaman Sea. It's here for a reason."

"Not anymore, it isn't," Matthew said, showing the radar screen. "The storm's finally gotten to be too much for the Yantar. She's pulling away. And we should too."

"All right," Tom said. "At least that's something. I feel better knowing that the Russian vessel can't do anything while this cyclone rages on."

"That might not be true," Elise said. "The *Yantar* just launched its deep-sea submersible."

CHAPTER FORTY-SEVEN

―――――⸻❖⸻―――――

Bottom of the Mariana Trench

SAM WATCHED THE SEAFLOOR MINING machine approach. Its massive dredge cutter head began to spin, feeding everything inside, in a guttural crushing sound. He suddenly understood what it felt like to be a small bug about to have its limbs gnawed off by a large praying mantis.

Nobody said a word.

There was nothing to say. Nothing to do. They were trapped and a machine designed to withstand the crushing pressure of 36,000 feet of water, and crush stones the size of cars, was slowly approaching them.

Sam held his breath.

The machine came to a stop directly in front of them. The driver of the vehicle could be seen working controls high up inside the safety of a domed compartment. He didn't look at them, and if he did, he didn't show any sign of recognition, while he continued to adjust the controls.

A single manipulator arm extended from the machine,

attaching itself to a hook on the side of *Ursula's* portside pontoon.

"The damned thing's latched onto us like a grappling hook!" Sam turned to Major Marazzato. "You still think this thing's from the future?"

Marazzato clenched his jaw, his arm holding the bracing bar tight. "I have no fucking idea!"

A moment later, the machine started to move.

Sam jerked backward into his seat with a jolt, as the submarine started moving. The seabed mining machine dragged them inside the sphere.

He watched as they slid in through the lockout chamber, before coming to a complete stop. The door closed, and they were trapped inside the sphere.

A blue haze from ambient lighting lit the room.

It turned red suddenly.

"What do you think the color changes mean?" Marazzato asked.

Sam thought about it for a second. "If this was a submarine, I'd say they're about to blow the ballast, dispelling the water and filling the room with air."

Marazzato shifted uncomfortably in his chair, as though eager to fight whoever was responsible for this. He turned to Dr. Smyth. "Does that make sense to you, doctor?"

Dr. Smyth sat with her hands folded across her lap, the only one among them who appeared fully calm, as though accepting whatever fate should fall her way. She shrugged. "I'm afraid submarines are more your area of expertise, Major."

Another few seconds passed, and the argument became moot.

Air bubbles filled the room, venting in from beneath them somewhere, expelling the water and filling the entire place with gas.

The million-dollar question being, was that gas breathable?

As soon as the water was cleared another door opened up, and the mining machine started to move again, disappearing down another tunnel, leaving them to their solitude.

All three of them waited another couple of minutes as though expecting someone else to come and tell them what to do.

Finally, Dr. Smyth said, "Shall we get out?"

Marazzato said, "The gas may not be breathable?"

Sam shrugged. "Then again, we're going to run out of air in another three days."

Dr. Smyth stood up, stretching as much as the shallow bubble would allow, her hands reaching up to the internal lock on the hatch.

"What are you doing?" Sam asked.

"I'm not waiting around any longer." She grinned. "I thought I might go stretch my legs outside."

"She's nuts!" Marazzato said.

"Does it matter?" Sam asked. "Let her go. We're going to be out of air soon enough anyway. If we're going to have to take a gamble, we may as well do it now. Here's to hoping the future US Navy still needed to breathe air."

He unlocked the latch and all three of them climbed out of the submarine.

Sam took a slow, deep, breath in through his nose. The air was cool. It had a distinct scent to it. Something out of place. Something he couldn't quite place at first. A strong scent of a forest. He took another deep breath. It was the scent of a pine forest.

Major Marazzato grabbed his backpack and followed them out.

Sam asked, "What the hell have you got that's so important in your bag."

Marazzato opened the top of the bag to reveal a bomb. "It's

nuclear."

Sam raised his eyebrows. "You brought a bomb to the bottom of the ocean. Are you insane?"

"Hey, I wasn't lying when I said we had no idea where this thing came from. One thing for certain it's a million miles more advanced than we are. This might be our only chance to destroy it. We need to take that chance. If you want to do something useful, why don't you have a look and see if you can work out how to open the lockout locker so we can escape."

Dr. Smyth raised a Beretta M9 handgun, aiming it directly at Major Marazzato. "I'm afraid that's not going to work out very good for anyone, Major."

Marazzato lifted the palms of his hands. "Hey, let's not do anything stupid here."

She smiled, the mischief still in her eyes, as she grinned. "That's exactly what I was going to say when you wanted to pull out a nuclear bomb."

Sam asked, "What do you want, doc?"

She pointed the Beretta to the right side of the chamber. "I want you both over there where I can see you. And Major, I suggest you leave the bomb where it is. No quick moves. I've won the US Pistol Shooting Association's national championships twice. I won't hesitate and I won't miss."

They backed away into the corner, Marazzato leaving his backpack behind.

Sam expelled a breath. "Now what?"

CHAPTER FORTY-EIGHT

On Board the *Tahila*

ELISE'S COMPUTER FLASHED RED.

Her program had found its first match.

She clicked the image, and her program brought up a man's face. He almost seemed familiar. Not someone she'd met, but more like someone she'd seen on a public forum. The face was a very near genetic match, meaning that he must be immediately related to one of the *Thirty* graduates.

She ran her eyes down to the man's name — Ryan Smith.

He was a sitting US Senator.

Elise brought up the Senator's details.

He was born in Texas, but orphaned at birth. He excelled at sports and in his schooling, gaining an SAT in the highest percentile, before moving to Massachusetts to study under a Fulbright Scholarship at MIT. There he studied engineering and went on to develop a number of patents under his name.

Within a decade, his talents had brought him riches beyond his dreams. He opened up an engineering company that went on to develop research that eventually led to the development of an MRI machine, cochlear implants, visual aids, and solid-state hard drives, that went on to be used in smartphones and most computers.

While he remained interested in engineering, he turned his focus toward politics, securing his position as a Senator in Connecticut.

Elise started to see through the web of lies.

But what had happened in the sixties?

Had the government really secured a team of the best engineers in the country? And if so, for what purpose? The world was in a state of crisis with the Cold War. Had the company locked up its brightest minds to develop a weapon?

If so, what happened to them?

Had Senator Ryan Smyth been the only survivor? Had he escaped, taking the team's enormous supply of technological achievements with him?

She looked at a photo of the man's family.

He had a child. A daughter named, Alyssa Smyth. She was grown up now, of course, and had a job as a Medical Director at the CDC.

Elise picked up her phone and dialed the Senator's personal cell number. It was an easy hack to get, having tapped into the phone accounts.

The Senator answered on the first ring. "Hello?"

"Senator Smyth?"

"Speaking."

"My name's Elise. I'm working a case with your daughter. She gave me your number and said you might be able to help me with something."

"Okay. What can I do for you ma'am?"

Elise held her breath. "Well sir, can you tell me about Habitat Zero."

CHAPTER FORTY-NINE

―――――⁌⁍―――――

Inside the Obsidian Sphere

PROFESSOR RAY SMYTH LEANED DOWN and blew out the candles.

It was his hundredth birthday today. A veritable feat, he thought, given that this entire thing started with the Cold War. It was nearly seventy years ago when the USSR and the USA were on the brink of nuclear war, when he came into command of Habitat Zero.

He looked upon the seven hundred odd people in the room and smiled. The muscles of his face tightly hanging across the skeletal frame of his once proud face. These were his people. His family. His friends. And what remains of the human race.

Only, the human race still existed outside.

A tear rolled down his cheek. It had been nearly a lifetime since he'd made the worst mistake of his life. Since he and a group of thirty intellectuals lied for the greatest purpose of all—to save the human race.

Habitat Zero was to be a shelter.

A nuclear bunker for humanity. Filled with the brightest minds of the time, selected based on their age, genetics, intelligence, and physical abilities, they joined a list of workers, totaling a community of just five hundred persons.

Given the worst-case scenario of all out nuclear war, Habitat Zero would provide shelter for a small gene pool of the best of humanity.

The obsidian sphere itself was provided by an ancient race, who had done a deal with President J.F. Kennedy.

To this day, he never learned what the president had traded.

In the end, what the sphere had asked of him — his soul.

He closed his eyes, as his mind retraced his history. They say the road to hell was paved with good intentions. But he wasn't so sure. There were plenty of times he could have chosen another path and the reason he didn't had nothing to do with good intentions.

If he wanted to keep lying to himself as he did to all those around him, he would say that he did it all to protect them, to save humanity. Sometimes good things require people to do terrible things. He swallowed down the guilt, looking at himself with the hard vision of a man who had reached 100 and knew that his time on Earth was short. The Nazis might have made the same argument when they murdered the Jews, disabled children, and the elderly.

He did it because he liked it.

And the only way to make it work was to sever ties with his own government.

He played the image out in his mind. The idea was that the sphere would be towed by a ship out to a secret location and then its seacocks — the oversized drains at the bottom of a boat — would be opened, and the hull flooded, so that the ship and the obsidian sphere would sink to the bottom. In doing so, no one from the surface would ever find them.

The idea was that the sphere would intermittently — twice a

year during summer and winter solstice — float a HF radio to the surface via an umbilical line and make a coded communication with the Pentagon.

They even kept in communications for some time, until there were talks that the Cold War was cooling down. The Soviets had lost their will for the fight. People had turned their attention to the space race.

The Pentagon had requested that the program be cancelled.

And Professor Ray Smyth permanently severed the umbilical line.

He told his people that the world above had indeed been destroyed. Nobody knows who fired first. But it no longer mattered who was to blame. The fact was, the world they had once known no longer existed, and it was up to them to survive long enough to see humanity survive.

It was this purpose which drove the men and women of Habitat Zero to continue. They worked hard, making improvements on biosphere technologies, computers, health, and science. When computers became vital to their progress, they built submersible mining machines to extract the vital materials needed to develop the microprocessors from the hydrothermal vents, including platinum, gold, and copper.

He wanted to succeed.

Truly, he believed in the cause, but in the 1960s, no technology was good enough to make a perfect biosphere, and soon it became apparent that they would eventually dissolve their progress and retreat into the dark ages, before starvation, infertility, and eventually death overcame their community.

Refusing to accept this, he sent his only son out into the world.

By sending him technology that they had developed, his son was able to build a tech engineering firm, which rapidly acquired many patents, quickly bringing in millions and eventually billions of dollars. Those dollars were spent purchasing new materials, equipment, and live animal stock to prop up his failing biosphere.

The sphere itself was designed to have four main agricultural rooms, in which animals could be moved from one to the other in an ongoing process to maintain the nutrients of any area. Smyth would then re-introduce new animals where need be in a secluded area, while the majority in Habitat Zero were no wiser.

With outside resources flowing in, Habitat Zero thrived.

Technology progressed faster than anywhere else on Earth. The brightest minds were all locked within a confined space, driven by the goal to save humanity, and in doing so they had overcome unbelievable challenges.

But as he looked out on all those smiling, happy faces, he felt nothing but guilt—for the lives that he stole.

"Is everything all right?" Someone asked.

He forced a smile. "Yes of course. I'm just a little nostalgic. That's all."

One of the miners came running into the obsidian cavern. The man was yelling loudly. People started yelling next to him, but Professor Smyth couldn't make out what they were saying.

He stood up and spoke with the booming voice of a commander. "I will have quiet in the chamber. Tell me," he said, looking at the miner. "What have you found?"

The miner was breathing hard. He stopped, leaning forward to catch his breath and said, "I found survivors!"

"What?"

"There were survivors on the seabed inside a submarine. I've brought them here!"

CHAPTER FIFTY

Sam looked at Dr. Smyth. "You want to tell us what's going on?"

Her brows furrowed. "An ancient race built this sphere so that humanity could survive in the event of a nuclear holocaust during the Cold War between the USSR and USA. My grandfather developed the biosphere technology to make it hospitable for upward of five hundred people."

Sam took in the obsidian walls. Of course the Master Builders were behind this. But he'd never known them to build a moving craft before. "How does it move?"

"It doesn't. It was towed here and then its ballast tanks opened so that it sank to the bottom. It's the obsidian that makes it so strong. It's built the same way a termite might build its nest, with hundreds of passages and tunnels, surrounded by a single core of energy. This unique heating system allows the sphere to regulate its temperature, with warm and cold areas flowing naturally throughout."

Sam asked, "What sort of energy system have kept them alive all this time?"

"Nuclear fusion."

"You mean, nuclear fission?" Sam clarified. "The same sort of system you have on a nuclear-powered submarine—it's used to propel the vessel and also to run the electrolysis which extracts oxygen from water molecules..."

Dr. Smyth smiled. "No. I meant fusion. You don't really think that I as a nuclear expert I would mix the two concepts up, do you?"

"Nuclear fusion!" Sam said, his eyes widening. "That's the holy grail of energy source. True energy. But it's a myth! Just a theory. Something for the future."

Marazzato said, "What the hell's nuclear fusion?"

Sam said, "Fusion power is—or was—a theoretical form of power generation in which energy will be generated by using nuclear fusion reactions to produce heat for electricity generation. In a fusion process, two lighter atomic nuclei combine to form a heavier nucleus, and at the same time, they release energy. This is the same process that powers stars like our Sun. It uses hydrogen isotopes such as deuterium and tritium, which react more easily, and create a confined plasma of millions of degrees using inertial methods. The main benefit of the process is that it will provide much more energy than traditional forms of nuclear power, while releasing very little nuclear waste byproducts."

"Sounds great," Marazzato said. "So what's the problem?"

"It doesn't work." Sam shrugged. "Okay, it didn't work, until now. Basically, research into fusion reactors began in the 1940s, but with the exception of the one at the center of Habitat Zero, to date, no design has produced more fusion power output than the electrical power input. But no one could work it out. So how did your grandfather get a hold of it?"

"The ancient ones gave us nuclear fusion."

Sam looked at her, she was still holding a gun at him. "Only you?"

"President John F. Kennedy to be exact."

"Why?"

"They had a deal."

Major Marazzato shook his head emphatically. "What sort of damned deal?"

"There's an ancient race… that live beneath the sea somewhere…"

Sam said, "We call them the Master Builders. They've been around for more than a hundred thousand years. They are genetically Homo Sapiens, but they have some anomalies that prevent them from aging very quickly. Unfortunately for them, this genetic fault, has led to a decrease in their fertility rates."

"That's right, they're dying out."

Sam said, "It's been happening for thousands of years."

"It's getting worse. They're getting desperate."

"And so they made a deal with President JFK?"

"They needed to keep performing genetic experiments on Homo Sapiens."

"JFK traded the Master Builders humans for technology?"

"No. The Master Builders already had a small pool of roughly twenty thousand unevolved Homo Sapiens."

Sam gasped. "The 8th Continent!"

"I see you're better informed than me." She made a wry smile. "So the Master Builders traded their technology so that JFK would agree to keep the 8th Continent hidden. The submerged continent doesn't appear on any satellite images, maps, or shipping routes."

"It's seems like one hell of a gift to trade for something so simple."

Dr. Smyth made a coy smile. "There was one other thing the Master Builders needed. Something that they couldn't access themselves."

"What?"

"A rare element found at the bottom of the Mariana Trench. It sometimes floated up to the surface and could be harvested, but they needed it in greater numbers, and to do that they needed someone to go down there and get it."

Sam asked, "Why couldn't they do it themselves?"

"There aren't more than twenty Master Builders left alive in the world. That means they don't have the human resources to do it. Besides, the Master Builders have always been the brains of an operation, not the workers. They designed the pyramids, they didn't build it themselves."

"What's so important about the element?"

"It makes people feel good."

"So does heroin," Sam said. "What makes this drug any different?"

"It has no side effects, and it makes people happy simply existing."

Sam's lips curled upward with understanding. "That's how the Master Builders have kept their cohort of unevolved Homo Sapiens happy!"

"Exactly. Only, six months ago, you discovered the 8th Continent, and its waters were placed on the protected list, making it hard for us to deliver the elements. Then, the nearby volcano erupted destroying a uranium processing plant, and sending an island of pumice to the surface."

Sam said, "It was your people who killed the crew of the *Carpe Diem*?"

"No. That wasn't us. I believe it was one of the Master Builders who arranged it, afraid that the island would—as it did—lead to their processing plant being discovered."

Sam said, "There's one thing I don't understand?"

"Shoot."

"Why did you let us come down here in the first place?"

She smiled. "Because although my family came from Habitat

Zero, and my father got rich out of it, we've never been able to locate it. It was almost a myth. I had to know the truth."

"And now that you know it, what will you do?"

She swallowed. "I don't know. I didn't ask for any of this to happen. I believe in the concept of Habitat Zero. In the hope that its technology might bring for the future of humanity. But it's not up to me. It all depends what the people inside the sphere say when they find out the truth."

"They don't know?" Marazzato asked, his voice incredulous. "What did they think they were doing down here?"

"They thought the world above had been destroyed by a nuclear war."

Marazzato laughed now. "Oh boy. They're going to be pissed when they find out they've been trapped down here for seventy years, producing technology to make your family rich!"

The sound of footsteps moving along the obsidian passages echoed through the obsidian vault. More than a hundred people filled the room. They all looked like they had just come from a 1950s or 1960s dress up party. The men were in suits with ties or Navy dress uniform, and the women wore full length skirt and tight bodice, with a slightly above the knee hemline. The men were handsome and the women beautiful, with short cropped hair or long straight styles.

A man in a white US Navy's full-dress uniform introduced himself as Commander Baxter, the Commander of the Sphere.

There were tears of joy and happiness.

Everyone started hugging. People were asking about where they had come from. Who else had survived? What was left of the world above? Were there any other survivors? Can people still see the blue sky or is there a permanent cloud of nuclear dust?

But before any answers were given, someone ran into the room, and meeting the commander's eyes, said, "Commander, another submarine has just docked on the eastern lockout locker!"

"Another submarine... one of yours?" Sam asked the Commander.

The Commander shook his head, "We don't have any submarines that go to the surface."

Dr. Smyth turned to Sam, and asked, "Could it be one of yours?"

"No. *Ursula's* the only sub we have on board."

"What about another ship?" she asked. "Would your crew have arranged for a rescue submarine?"

"No way. There are no rescue submarines for this depth! Besides, the only subs that could reach this depth are thousands of miles away."

Marazzato said, "That might not be the case."

"What are you saying?" Sam asked.

"Before I cut the communications cable, there was a note on the communications computer from Elise on the surface. She warned that the *Yantar* was on the surface."

"Are you kidding me!" Sam said. "You didn't think to mention that the Russian spy vessel was tracking us?"

Marazzato crossed his arms. "Hey, I figured there was nothing we could do about it, so no reason to make the things any more stressful."

Sam turned to the Commander. "Sir, do you have any weapons on board?"

"Weapons?" The commander asked, his voice soft, almost surprised by the question. "There's an armory toward the center of the sphere next to the command center. Why?"

Sam met his eyes. "Because whatever submarine just docked with Habitat Zero it's crewed by an elite force of Russians."

CHAPTER FIFTY-ONE

Sam, Marazzato, and Dr. Smyth followed the Commander of the Habitat Zero at a run through the obsidian passageway heading toward the armory at the center of the sphere.

Sam said to the Commander "Can you secure the passageways and doors between the lockout chamber any the rest of the sphere?"

"Sure, there's a security code for everything we have. Although it's not used very often. In fact, I don't understand how they got in through the lockout chamber. It has a security code, too."

To Dr. Smyth, Sam said, "If the Master Builders weren't getting what they needed from Habitat Zero they would have searched for another trade partner."

"Oh shit!" Dr. Smyth swore. "They've reached out to the Russians."

"Exactly. The Russians have the access codes!"

The commander radioed his main security room. He made a quick exchange with his crew and then said to Sam, "There were twenty people on board the submarine. They unlocked the security doors, and have now split up into two groups."

The obsidian passageways were like a honeycomb maze of tunnels. They reached the armory. It was small, designed to take on a small group from a submarine in the unlikely event of an attack — not a group of twenty Russian elite forces.

A security officer had already unlocked the door and was handing out Stoner M63 assault rifles and ammunition. The weapons were state of the art, designed by DARPA in 1963, and went on to become the back bone of the future AR-15 and M16.

Sam examined the weapon.

It was in poor condition and had rarely been serviced in nearly seventy years. The Stoner 63 utilized a common receiver core to which various feeds, barrels, shoulder stocks, and other components were attached to configure the weapon's in-the-field service. Internally, the system still relied on the proven gas-operated, rotating bolt action — an arrangement that went on to be used in the AR-15 — but right now, Sam doubted if any of the weapons would fire, let alone allow them to take on an elite force of Russian soldiers.

Sam said to the officer, "You need to let everyone know you're under attack! They need to grab whatever weapons they have and defend Habitat Zero. The Russian soldiers are trying to take control of the sphere!"

"We don't have many weapons on board!"

"Then I suggest you'd better prepare for some casualties." Sam frowned. "Do you have a map?"

The officer rolled out a security map of the sphere. There were hundreds of passageways, tunnels, ladders, and downward slides. The entire thing looked like one big game of snakes and ladders.

The officer pointed to where the Russians had attacked. "If they keep heading downward, searching for the central command center, they will pass through this narrow funnel here. If we can stop the attack there, then we'll be fine."

Sam stared at the map. There were multiple routes leading in and away from that main conduit. It would be a hard place to hold and there didn't appear to be any cover.

"Make sure you tell your men to run from the attackers and not put up a fight until they get to that point there. We want to lull our attackers into a false sense of invincibility. They probably assume that after seventy years, no one has bothered to maintain any weapons."

"Okay, I'll let them know."

Sam glanced at his dusty old weapon and then at the armorer. "I don't suppose you have anything bigger?"

The armorer grinned. "As a matter of fact, I do."

CHAPTER FIFTY-TWO

S AM STARED AT THE 1963, General Electric, M134 minigun.

The massive weapon fired 7.62×51mm NATO shots via a six-barrel rotary machine gun with a high rate of fire capable of achieving 6,000 rounds per minute. Its external Gatling-style rotating barrels used an external electric power source. The weapon was designed to be mounted on the side of a helicopter or aircraft, but this one was on a wheeled tripod with shield.

Sam glanced at the map. "Can we get it moved to this point, here?"

The officer nodded. "Yeah, we can do that."

Within ten minutes, a small team had maneuvered the weapon into place at a small fork in the tunnel, overlooking the section of the main descending passageway as it funneled into a narrow section.

Sam stared at the video surveillance TV monitor. It was one of those old box-shaped TVs that took two people to carry and displayed the video in black and white.

The attacking soldiers were moving quickly.

Sam grinned.

Commander Baxter said, "What?"

"I'm sorry it's nothing. I've just never seen a black and white TV before."

"What color do your TVs show back home?"

Sam said, "Well… all of them."

The Commander shook his head. "Yeah, well, in case you hadn't heard, we've had a few more priority things to overcome in the past seventy years since we've been down here and making better TV entertainment wasn't one of them."

Sam and Major Marazzato set the minigun up so that it would kill anyone who came through, while a team of forty plus US Navy sailors, armed with Stoner M63s, took cover at the edge of every tunnel leading toward the funnel.

The Russian elite soldiers weren't expecting any defense. They moved with the confidence of the school yard bully, surrounded by their henchmen, but they were running toward their deaths. The Russians had been told that the sphere was run by a bunch of nerds from the sixties and that although they would be outnumbered, it would be easy to take control of the sphere's command center.

They were wrong.

The Russians ran into the funnel.

And Major Marazzato opened fire, while Sam fed the bullet-belt.

The minigun's massive Gatling-style external rotating barrels started to whir as their electric motor sent the barrel turning.

7.62×51mm NATO shots fired at a rate of 6,000 rounds per minute.

Sending a deadly barrage into the confined space of the narrowed tunnel.

The entire battle was over before it had begun.

Nearly half the Russian attackers died in the first few

seconds, while the others—taken by surprise by the overwhelming firepower response—turned and fled.

Marazzato fired another round of shots and then stopped.

Commander Baxter yelled, "After them, men!"

CHAPTER FIFTY-THREE

Command Center, Pentagon

GENERAL PAINTER STARED AT THE satellite image of the Pacific Ocean, south of Guam, where Sam Reilly and his crew had taken a submarine to the sphere below, three days ago. A Udaloy II Class Russian Destroyer, accompanied by the spy ship *Yantar* were visible through the fading cyclonic clouds in the north, while to the south, the *Tahila* and the *USS Michael Monsoor*, a Zumwalt Class Destroyer waited for their orders.

The President had been briefed about the historical role of Habitat Zero.

The President examined the satellite footage. "General Painter, what's your take on this?"

"It's dangerous, Mr. President." General Painter kept his chin up high, portraying confidence and pride as he spoke, and suppressing whatever fear he might have felt. "We and the Russians have high stakes in this. We have Sam Reilly, Dr. Smyth, and Major Marazzato potentially trapped down there, as well as the advanced technology of the sphere. While the

Russians have their own boarding crew still down there either on the submarine or potentially already inside the sphere."

The President arched his eyebrow. "You think that's possible?"

"We can't rule it out. The original sphere had the ability to be accessed through two systems similar to the lockout chambers on our nuclear submarines."

"So. What do you think our best response is?" The President stood up, focusing on the image of the four ships.

General Painter held his breath. "Sir, I think the only response we have is destroy the sphere. Now, traditional weapons won't pierce its obsidian hull. Therefore, I would suggest a specially modified nuclear warhead, fixed to an armor piercing torpedo. Now we could run a tether…"

"How many people do we have down there, General?"

"Just the three."

The President's eyes narrowed. "And the Russians?"

"Twenty."

The Secretary of Defense spoke up, her voice sharp and emphatic. "There's still the possibility that sphere has five hundred American men and women."

The President turned to General Painter. "Could that be true?"

General Painter bit down the fear that churned in his gut. "No, Mr. President. The last communication we received from the crew of Habitat Zero was in October 22, 1963. If they are still alive down there, you'd have to wonder, why they haven't made contact?"

The President ran his eyes across the rest of the members of his statutory attendees. His Vice President, Secretary of State, Secretary of Defense, Secretary of Energy, Secretary of the Treasury. Their faces all showed steely resolve.

"All right," the President said, "Let's take out the sphere."

Susan Borg, his Secretary of State, warned, "That might trigger a conflict between us and the Russians."

"Margaret?" he asked, turning to meet his Secretary of Defense directly. "What do you think?"

"I think that analysis is highly unlikely, sir. You can get around any mishaps, simply by contacting the Russians directly, and advising them that you plan to destroy the sphere, which is one of our own vessels. No one can argue that you were trying to enrage war, when you shoot down your own vessel."

The President arched an eyebrow. "So you approve of the idea?"

"No, sir. My concern isn't about escalating to war with the Russians. My concern is entirely for our own people. There have been reports that the original colony of people on Habitat Zero are still alive."

"That might be true, and it might not be." The President liked to walk around the room when he addressed the committee. "The point becomes moot here. You see, one thing we know for certain, inside that sphere, there we have more advanced technology than anywhere else in the world. If we do nothing, the Russians will board the sphere and take command of it. Once that happens, we will be well outside our grounds to destroy the damned thing." He changed his tact, as though the committee's acceptance of his speech, a foregone conclusion. "All right, any other concerns?"

No one spoke.

"Good. General Painter, make the arrangements. I want the sphere nuked."

"Yes, Mr. President."

CHAPTER FIFTY-FOUR

Live Video Feed from the USS Michael Monsoor

Inside the Pentagon Command Center, the Secretary of Defense breathed hard as she watched the live feed coming in from the *USS Michael Monsoor*.

There was silence in the room.

The decision to destroy the sphere had already been made. Now it was merely a case of waiting and watching as the fine men and women of the US Navy implemented the decision.

She watched the torpedo fire.

Given the extremely devastating power it was about to commit, the little torpedo — at just 19 feet in length and 21 inches in diameter — seemed surprisingly small as it whirred its way through the water before turning its head vertical and nose diving toward the sphere.

The nuclear torpedo was tethered to the *USS Michael Monsoor* via a communication cable, which provided real-time data including its built-in sonar and video feed.

The video feed became useless after three thousand feet when it entered the ocean's midnight zone and everything became dark.

The sonar continued to show what little was in front of the torpedo as it raced to the bottom of the Mariana Trench.

Traveling at a speed of 55 knots, it took just over 6.1 minutes to reach the sphere.

The Secretary of Defense involuntarily held her breath as the sphere came into visual range of the torpedo's sonar.

On the top left-hand corner of the video feed, a number showed the reducing distance in feet between the torpedo and the sphere.

It entered the last 1000 feet.

The Secretary of Defense fixed her eyes on the sphere, praying that Sam Reilly and his crew had gotten out and that she had been wrong about the original crew of the Habitat Zero program.

A moment later, the sphere disappeared.

The torpedo circled around the location where the sphere had been and then stopped, leaving a visual feed of the sonar view of the seafloor below.

The President stood up, and turning to General Painter for clarity, said, "What the hell just happened?"

General Painter said, "We're working on it, Mr. President. It might just be a fault with the communications cable. Maybe our live-feed has frozen."

The feed showed the torpedo was circling in a classic predator-prey attack mode, searching for and trying to acquire its target.

The Secretary of Defense shook her head. "That doesn't look like a video-feed issue to me."

The President said, "Then, do you want to tell me what the hell happened to my damned sphere!"

"I think it's obvious, Mr. President."

"What?" he replied, in an unrestrained voice.

The Secretary of Defense straightened the hem of her suit. "Well sir, I believe the crew from Habitat Zero are still alive, and they just took evasive maneuvers to avoid being destroyed."

The President's eyes narrowed. "But Habitat Zero never had its own propulsion system… it was towed out into the Pacific and then sunk to the bottom of the Mariana Trench."

The Secretary of Defense suppressed a grin. "It appears, sir, the crew have upgraded Habitat Zero."

CHAPTER FIFTY-FIVE

On Board the *Tahila*-Caribbean Sea

SAM REILLY WATCHED THE NEWS report he'd been waiting for.

The members of the United Nations had banded together to reprimand the Russian government after investigations revealed a large-scale nuclear waste storage facility had been discovered beneath the Andaman Sea off the coast of Thailand and Myanmar. It had been used for nearly sixty years to dispose of nuclear waste.

Sam watched it with pleasure.

The next report showed Commander Baxter speaking to a group of News Reporters. It had now been two weeks since Habitat Zero had officially declared its independence from the United States of America. Its commander stated that his committee believed that seeing as the sphere had been run as an Independent state for more than seventy years, without any acknowledgement or aid from the United States, it was entitled to now be recognized as such.

During the report, the Commander noted that they had just

delivered their letter of such intent to the Security Council of the United Nations, asking for admission to the UN.

Sam grinned.

They would have an uphill battle trying to secede from the United States. It was a battle he didn't envy them. Nor did he believe it mattered what he thought they should do. The fact was, they had been lied to for nearly seventy years. There were children on board who were now in their late sixties, who had never seen the sun, let alone, been to the United States.

It all made for a horrible situation.

But he was pleased that the people of Habitat Zero had come through with the strength and resilience to let the world know what they want.

His phone rang.

It was the Secretary of Defense. "Did you watch the news?"

"Yes," Sam said, noncommittally.

"Wasn't that a nightmare," she said. "Don't they know they're going to have hell to pay if they want their independence."

"Yeah, I figured," Sam said. "Just wait until the lawsuits start to flow. You know someone will still remember about the judicial system. Someone will want compensation. From what I hear, DARPA knew about Habitat Zero and was using its unique group of people to develop technology for them, through the use of their original Commander—a Mr. Ray Smyth—who had kept the entire population in the dark about the truth."

"Do you know what became of Mr. Smyth?" she asked, more out of curiosity than any professional purpose.

"He had a heart attack the day we arrived. It just so happened to be his birthday. But some might have said the guilt killed him—or maybe he simply accepted it was time for the truth to come out."

The Secretary of Defense said, "Yeah, well I'll admit that what happened was awful, but I still don't believe it gives them the right to their independence."

Sam looked out at the ocean, the freedom of the waves, and smiled. "On that subject, you know who else is going to apply for their independence?"

"Yes, I've already heard. The new government of the 8th Continent."

Sam grinned. "You know they're going to achieve it, too… don't you?"

"Yeah, that one can't be helped. Although I wouldn't be surprised if the British want to argue that it was traditionally one of their own colonies."

Sam laughed. "How do you figure that one?"

"What? Why not? The 8th Continent was once part of the Australian Continent."

"More than fifty thousand years ago."

"I don't know. Queen Elizabeth is weakening in her old age, but at her peak she never would have let one of her colonies escape."

Sam smiled. "Was there anything else you called about, Madam Secretary?"

"Yes. You will be happy to know Alicia Yeager woke up."

"Who?"

"Alicia Yeager. She was the woman you found on board the *Carpe Diem*. She was treated for acute radiation sickness. There was concern she wasn't going to wake up. But she did."

"How is she?"

"She's been better. She would like to thank you for saving her life."

Sam smiled. "I'm glad she's okay."

The Secretary of Defense ended the call.

A few minutes later he received another phone call.

He answered it on the third ring. It was a number he didn't

recognize.

But he recognized the soft Kansas accent of the woman on the other end. "Hello," he said.

"Hello, Mr. Sam Reilly."

"Sam will do fine, ma'am."

"All right, Sam. Do you know who I am?"

"Yes, ma'am. You're the fine young woman I met in the 8th Continent."

"That's right, although I don't know how accurate the young woman part is."

Sam let her comment slide.

She continued. "I've called to say thank you for your help. We're making an official attempt at our independence now that the previously ruling class have... how should I put it... abdicated their positions."

Sam smiled. "My connections tell me that you killed the previous leader."

"No. I deny that emphatically. We had the Gifted One — those who you call Master Builders — who managed the Summer Quadrant held under house arrest, nothing more."

"So what happened to him?"

"One of the other Master Builders killed him."

Sam's eyes narrowed. "Why would they do that?"

"I don't know. I'm told their entire race is dying out and they were worried about losing some of their most hidden secrets."

"You might be right."

"Anyway. I have a meeting in Washington to seek support and to discuss how we move forward with this thing…"

Sam asked, "You're going to be the President?"

"Goodness no. I'm afraid I'm passed that time in my life, but I would like to support the people of the 8th Continent. Their progress has been withheld for too many years."

Sam looked out at the rolling waves. "Let me know when you come to Washington. I don't know if there's all that much I can do to help your cause, but I'd like to meet up. Nothing inappropriate. Coffee or lunch or something. I'd just like to hear your stories."

"All right, I would like that."

"Oh, and Amelia…"

"Yes, Sam?" she replied without challenging him.

"I was serious when I said that I'd been enamored with you since I was a young boy."

There was silence on the phone.

Amelia's voice softened. "Mr. Reilly, are you flirting with me?"

"No, ma'am."

"Good. Because, despite what I might look like, I'm old enough to be your great grandmother."

Sam laughed. "You don't look a day over thirty-five."

"Yeah, well I sure feel a lot older."

"Good bye, Amelia."

"Good bye, Mr. Reilly."

EPILOGUE

British M15 Headquarters

His assistant said, "I'm afraid we've lost Excalibur."

Dexter's eyes narrowed. "Good God! Are you certain?"

"The evidence is compelling."

"But we shut down the project in 2011. Excalibur was to be put down."

"He was, but there was a complication."

Dexter nodded. "I remember. The vessel he was being transported on sank."

His assistant raised his eyebrows. "Yes. The report suggested a fire. But my guess is that Excalibur was behind it."

"You're kidding. He was sedated and restrained."

"What did you think he was going to do? He knew he was being sent to his execution. You didn't think he would let that happen so easily?"

Dexter nodded. "Sure, but the ship sank in the end. There were no survivors."

"You're forgetting Excalibur was one hell of a swimmer."

"Sure, but out there in the middle of the ocean. How long could he have survived?"

"Long enough to reach the Oregon Coast."

Dexter coughed. "You mean, as in the US West Coast?"

His assistant crossed his arms. "Afraid so."

"That can't be an accident."

"No. It would appear not."

Dexter picked up the report and fingered through the notes. "What's he doing there?"

His assistant met his eye. "You know what he's doing there."

Dexter nodded. Breathing heavily. "Have you contacted Dr. Peterson, to warn him?"

"Yes."

Dexter raised his eyebrows. "How did he take that?"

"How do you think he took that? What would you do if you discovered Excalibur had survived and was spotted on his way to find you?"

"I'd run."

"Exactly."

"Did he?" Dexter asked, his voice almost hopeful.

His assistant remained silent for a moment. "No. Dr. Patterson said there was nowhere on Earth he would ever be safe while Excalibur was alive. Better that he bunkers down at his place, and rolls the dice. Live or die. There's a team of US Rangers — Delta Force I believe — on their way now to help."

"Did you tell them what they're up against?" There was an urgency in Dexter's voice.

"Of course I did."

"And?"

His assistant placed the palms of his hands skyward. "They didn't believe me. How could they? If the roles were reversed, would you?"

Dexter thought about that for a second. His shoulders slumped forward. "No."

"That's right. And now they're flying into a trap."

"How many men?"

"Twenty. Two choppers. Two teams. They might be enough."

Dexter expelled a deep breath of air. "God help them. They have no idea what they're up against."

His assistant's cell phone rang. It made him jump with a start. He answered it on the second ring. "Yes?"

His assistant listened for a while. His face turning ashen gray. Finally he said, "Yes, I understand."

Dexter swallowed. "What is it?"

"That was the Commanding Officer of the US Ranger's Delta Force strike team. They just arrived at the doctor's house."

"And... what did they find?"

"Dr. Patterson's dead. His body was carved with surgical precision into small pieces and then set up to look like it was laughing at them all, like some sort of sick joke."

The muscles around Dexter's lips tightened into a grimace. He felt his gut churn. "Really?"

"That's what the Ranger said." His assistant sighed. "It's the sort of thing Excalibur would do."

Dexter sighed. "You're right, some weapons can't be destroyed."

"There's something else you should know."

"What?"

"They found a note written in the doctor's blood."

Dexter said, "Go on. What did it say?"

His assistant bit his lower lip, gritted his teeth. He expelled a deep breath of air. "It said, *You're next, Dexter.*

Dexter was silent.

His assistant asked, "What are you going to do, sir?"

Dexter remained silent. His mind ticking over like clockwork. Every answer returning to the same conclusion. If he stayed, he would be dead.

"Do we come clean about the project?" his assistant asked.

Dexter shook his head emphatically. "Oh God, no! We'll have civil rights groups from around the world breathing down our neck. No. We destroy all records that from that part of the program and shut it down for good."

"What about Excalibur?"

Dexter swallowed. "You mean, do we go after him again?"

"Yeah."

"No. You saw what the program did to a goddam dog? There's no end of imagining what Excalibur's capable of."

"Yeah, you're right. So what are you going to do?"

Dexter sighed. "The same thing any sane man would do. I'm going to do what Dr. Peterson couldn't. I'm going to work out how to run."

THE END

Want more?

Join my email list and get a FREE and EXCLUSIVE Sam Reilly story that's not available anywhere else!

Join here ~ www.bit.ly/ChristopherCartwright

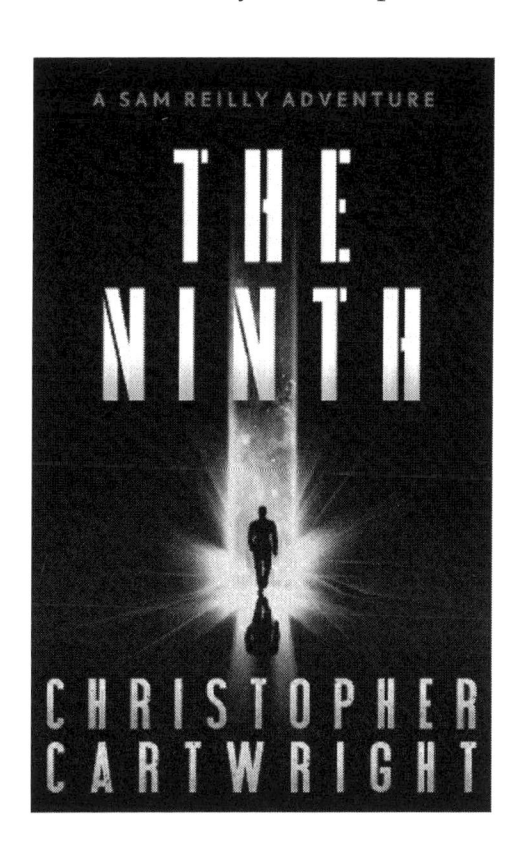